TRUE GHOST STORIES OF CONNECTICUT

TRUE GHOST STORIES OF CONNECTICUT

TRUE GHOST STORIES OF CONNECTICUT

Hauntings, Spirits, Creatures, Cryptids, Entities,
the Occult, the Paranormal, and the Supernatural

**First-Hand Paranormal Accounts by Individuals
Who Experienced the Occurrences**

BY "CRYPTMASTER CHUCKY"
Charles F. Rosenay!!!

Forward by
The Amazing Kreskin

TRUE GHOST STORIES OF CONNECTICUT

© 2022 Charles F. Rosenay!!! All Rights Reserved.

No part of this book may be reproduced or transmitted in any form or by means electronic or mechanical, including photocopying or information retrieval system, without permission in writing from the publisher. Permission is granted to other publications or media to excerpt the contents for review purposes, provided that the proper and correct credit and copyright information is included for any materials reproduced.

The images and photos included in this book are © of their respective copyright holders and are presented herein with permission or as Fair Use to be illustrative for the text held. The material in this book is intended for historical purposes and literary criticism, review, and accounts are used by permission.

There is no affiliation, endorsement, or connection between any of the contributors and this book and its author.

Layout by Michael A. Ventrella

Published in the USA.
ISBN: 978-1-93576-823-4

kiwi·publishing

TRUE GHOST STORIES OF CONNECTICUT

TABLE OF CONTENTS

Dedication..9
Foreword
    by The Amazing Kreskin..11
Welcome to the Spirits: Introduction
    by Charles F. Rosenay!!!..17
Carousel Gardens with The Warrens
    by Jimmy "Mr. Haunted" Petonito................................29
Chris Mark Castle in Woodstock
    by Christine and Daniel Peer..34
Dark Siege: A Connecticut Family's Nightmare
    by Jason McLeod..40
Derby's Sterling Opera House
    by Rich DiCarlo..43
Derby's Sterling Opera House: More Proof of the Paranormal
    by Margaret Scholz..53
Down in the Valley: Beyond the Opera Houses
    by Michael James Mascolo..57
Drawing Out The Ansonia Opera House Phantoms
    by Charles F. Rosenay!!!..65
Dudleytown Experience
    by Lisa Marie McKinney..68
Dudleytown Revisited
    by Charles F. Rosenay!!!..71
Fairfield Hills Asylum
    by Nick Grossmann..74
Green Lady Cemetery
    by Tommy Dreivers..79
Haunted at Home
    by Paul Longo Jr..81
Haunted by History: The Curtis House
    by Leanna Renee Hieber..85
Hookman's Cemetery
    by Jeffrey Gerry..89
Meeting Ed and Lorraine Warren
    by Steve Biff Saunders..92

Middletown's Connecticut Valley Hospital
   by Anthony Mullin.. 95
My Warrens Story
   by Charles F. Rosenay!!!.. 98
New Canaan's Possessed Lady
   by Hector Roque...101
New-Gate Prison
   by Larry and Debbie Elward.. 103
Night at the Conjuring House
   by Larry and Debbie Elward.. 105
On Nova Scotia Hill
   by Angela Marie.. 108
One Twisted Night at The Twisted Vine
   by Margaret Scholz..111
Phantom Messages
   by Bill Hall.. 112
Robbins Swamp, East Canaan: Bigfoot!
   by Colin Haskins and the CCIS Team................................... 115
Seaside Shadows
   by Rich Cyr... 119
Seymour: A Different Kind of Howling
   by Diane Berti... 123
Stratford's Portal Lady
   by Nick Grossmann... 124
The Egyptian Cryptid at New Haven's Center Church
   by Chrystyne McGrath... 130
The Hospital
   by Kathy Chruszcz... 132
The Litchfield Slaying
   by Betsy-ann Rosenberg.. 136
The New Demon House of Derby
   by Mike Cronin... 138
The Old Pine Tree
   by John Zaffis..141
The Pink Lady of New Haven
   by Charles F. Rosenay!!!.. 144
And Finally
   by Charles F. Rosenay!!!.. 149

Index.. 153

DEDICATION

I dedicate this book to The Warrens, the paranormal pioneers of Connecticut. They have paved the way for so many ghosthunters and investigators.

I also dedicate this book to all those who have made paranormal investigating their lives and their passion, whether in Connecticut or elsewhere.

Thank you to all the contributors to this book, and Special Thanks to Nick Grossmann (brutha) for leading me on this wild and wonderful journey.

Most importantly, thank you to the greatest loves of my life:
My wife Melissa and our children Lauren, Harrison, and Ian.

FOREWARD

by The Amazing Kreskin

The concept of recounting various incidents that seem unexplainable is one that I know will be handled with great skill and fascination by Charles Rosenay!!! and his contributors to this book. The paranormal has played a major role in my career, and you're going to find that Rosenay!!! and his colleagues' reflections and examinations of the field are going to be spellbinding.

I predicted a couple of years ago that there will soon be a time of renewed interest in the various incidents that are considered paranormal phenomena, whether we call it ESP, telepathy, paranormal cognition, etc., since it deals with people's fascinating experiences and capacity to examine unexplained phenomena that just doesn't seem to be understandable at the present moment.

Séances were very popular in the earlier part of the last century, and it became a fascinating area for sophisticated people who wanted to experiment by having séances in the home. There was no television, radio had not come into the picture yet, and it was a wonderful, very popular excuse and opportunity to communicate in a dramatic fashion. I have, just a few years ago, stated that there would be, when the pandemic calms down, a renewed interest in paranormal experiences, whether one believes in it or feels that there is a scientific explanation available to them, or is simply unknown phenomena.

Let me point out that, at times, my work as a performer has dealt with almost unexplained phenomena that I was able to produce on stage. I do not call myself a psychic, I do not make extravagant claims, but at the same time, I have a right to express my own personal opinion about my skills, and my position is that I feel very strongly that I have been born with a genuine gift. It is a gift that I cannot fully explain, but one which has been dramatic and will carry me through my entire career. In the twenty-two books I have written, they have been a result of the tremendous and extensive experiences that I have had, some of which I could not explain, but experiences are many since the estimates of even the travel part of my career is that I have flown over 3½ million miles.

Charles Rosenay!!! understands the fascination that you—my dear reader—have for the various happenings that are recounted as paranormal experiences. For one thing, part of the reason for an awakening in interest in unexplained phenomena is that man needs to again expand his range of communications since at times a search for the unexplained requires an extension of our minds and our willingness to open our thinking and widen our perspective on the happenings in and around our lives. This willingness to expand will result in awakening greater energies than we are even aware of. This is not to imply supernaturalism, but again the suggestion of some paranormal activity can't be ignored even if that activity a century from now is no longer categorized as paranormal.

Let me share with you one of the most memorable incidents of which I have no explanation at all on how it could have taken place.

It happened some decades ago, perhaps 30 to 40 years back, as I recall. I travel a great deal as I made clear earlier, and this incident took place in a travel setting that was unusual for me. I was on tour and my road manager was under the weather and was not able to accompany me on this trip. I'm usually on tour with a professional road manager who oversees the luggage, connections, and that the scheduling is fulfilled. It enables the performer to, of course, concentrate on his presentation and not on all the details of traveling.

Photos of Charles F. Rosenay!!! ("Cryptmaster Chucky") with The Amazing Kreskin at the "NYC FAB 50" Beatles' 50th Anniversary Celebration at Town Hall in New York, February, 2014

For some reason, I overslept this one morning when I was to fly out of Newark Airport in NJ later in the day to get to a performance in NY state. It was not extremely distant, but it was a flight itinerary that was well established. No road manager, and me oversleeping, was not the norm. To this day I wonder what in the world made me oversleep. It's not a habit and not a problem I suffer from. I ate a rapid fast-food breakfast, I found myself on my way, jumping into my car to the airport. For some inanely strange reason I decided to take a detour. Mind you, practically all my trips to the airport were not even navigated by yours truly, but I found myself going a different way and I was soon traveling through downtown Newark, which I looked back on with regret as the traffic was heavy and I wasn't used to shortcuts and what have you.

Finally, I was out of the city, driving to the airport. In those days you could park yourself, carry your own luggage through the terminal, check your bags in and security was not as great, and not as needed as it is today. I rushed up to the check-in counter, not needing to go through any examination, as they recognized me since I was flying out of Newark several days a week. They told me I could get to the flight by going down a certain hallway and the entrance to the flight would be there. I put my luggage on the conveyor belt, and it was taken to be placed on the jet.

I filled out a couple of forms, and they said, "Kreskin, you'd better hurry" (they all knew me). I said yes, and I explained that I was delayed in getting here. I rushed with one attaché case down the long corridor toward my departing gate, and when I arrived, I got there just in time to see my flight pulling away from the gate, a few feet from where I was standing. I had missed my flight.

I went back to the airline counter, where they realized I had missed my flight. They apologized , not knowing if I could have made the flight. They said there was another flight with a short connection, and that it would get me to the city where I needed to be. They changed the ticketing and I boarded my alternate flight not long after the one I missed. I flew on to another city, connected to my other flight and went on my way to the town in which I was working.

Thank goodness everything seemed to go smoothly. That evening I was by myself, and I had a stage crew who handled sound and lighting.

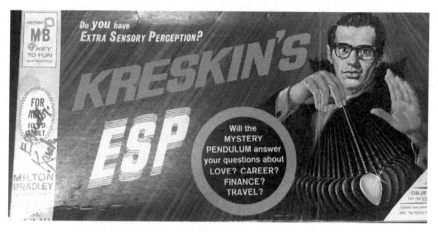

The show was sold out. I had simply set the stage with a few items, a table, a few chairs—all the basic items that I would use during my performance—and I was waiting backstage. They told me I had a very short amount of time before the show was about to start, and then my introduction was going to be announced by a speaker off of the stage. I was still in my dressing room as the introduction began, and when he stated my name as Kreskin, I would simply walk out and begin my performance, except it didn't begin.

There was a knock on my dressing room door.

This didn't make sense to me, as the crew, the staff at the theater, and everyone all knew I was scheduled to go on and it would not make sense to interrupt literally moments before the intro of me going in front of the audience. Why would they interrupt and break down the continuity of the show? I went to the door because they were trying to shake it open.

When I opened the door, I was looking at two police officers. They came into the dressing room and said, "You're Kreskin?" I said I was. They said, "We found that you were here because your luggage had a destination tag on it, but also a phone number to your office in NJ."

I said, "I don't understand," and they continued, "Kreskin, is this your luggage?" My response was yes, that I recognized it. The police said, "We hoped we'd be helpful because your luggage was discovered off of farmland in NY State as the plane had crashed and much of the contents of the flight was all over the place and we found this and wanted you to have this."

Well folks, my dear readers, there was a delay before I went on stage. I felt it was a perfect time and appropriate to change my clothes, and dress in my stage tuxedo and I walked out on stage. You could hear a pin drop in the theater for it certainly was one of the most mellow dramatic readings I've ever made with an audience. I pointed out to them that I missed my flight, and the flight I was supposed to be on crashed, and my luggage came to my dressing room thanks to the police. What made me miss my flight, oversleep, take the wrong route, delay what have you, resulting in my missing a major crash is a mystery I have never been able to even theoretically solve. There was no dream of a disaster, nothing negative, no sign or anything causing me to miss my flight, and yet, because of the delays, I was able to continue without any negative, damaging impact on my physical well being.

In my performances, especially my full evening concerts which run sometimes over two hours, I often dramatize mysterious moods and happenings that I can produce in the theater through the power of suggestion. Many a Halloween evening we've had a ball with a séance of some kind where a ghost seemed to be appearing in the theater and coming down the aisle. This is not to prove or create the existence of ghosts, but it was to illustrate how various influences can cause strange happenings to take place or appear to take place. As a result of this, whenever I include that in my performance, a ghost-like experience, we lock the doors of the theater until that scene is complete. The reason why is because in a performance some years ago in an Off-Broadway theater, one person was missing from a group that had volunteered on the stage and she was found 3 or 4 blocks down the street from the theater, rushing to avoid a ghostly happening which she saw. So now we take no chances by losing volunteers who chose to escape from dramatized artificial fears.

The fascination that I have is not only with the subject matter that Charles Rosenay!!! and his associates capture in their reminisces, but also in their varied writing styles. You could almost experience what they are relating to us, and I suspect that part of that is because they have become so familiar with a technique and skill of communicating without a visual support such as movies and television, leaving us with one of the most powerful forms of communication. I don't mean that simply in terms of news, but I'm speaking in terms of story-telling, remembrances, and recurring hauntings.

As an afterword to the foreword, my dear reader, if you get a chance, and this is a recommendation rarely given out, I suggest that after you finish this book you access Mr. Rosenay!!!'s first book, *The Book of Top 10 Horror Lists*. It is his collection of one hundred celebrities, including myself, offering their Top 10 favorite horror movies and themes. It is a refreshing departure and you will find it a unique addition to this current book which you are about to read.

The Amazing Kreskin
May 2022

INTRODUCTION: WELCOME TO THE SPIRITS

by Charles F. Rosenay!!!

For years, I have been the organizer and host of ghost-themed travel adventures. What does that mean? As a tour operator, I created and promoted theme tours for niche crowds. I produce Beatles Tours to Liverpool for Beatles fans, and I also present Dracula Tours to Transylvania. Yes, the real place —Transylvania, in Romania. Starting with our first "vampire vacation" in 1998, travelers from all over would journey with us to Transylvania for an adventure that mixed the legend and myths of Dracula with the truth and history of Vlad (Tepes) The Impaler. If I say so myself, the trip was (and still is) incredible. Travelers spend a week visiting all the sites and castles on a fully escorted, professionally-guided tour, which for years included an overnight stay in Dracula's Castle. They literally followed the footsteps of Jonathan Harker from Bram Stoker's novel *Dracula*. There aren't too many things in this world that generate 100% customer satisfaction, but these vacations were loved by all, so much so that the travelers asked for more similar trips, which inspired me to package GHOSTours to other destinations.

On one of my GHOSTours to England, I dressed as the sinister "Witchfinder General"

Our "tours of terror" took travelers to England (several times), Scotland, Ireland, Germany, the Czech Republic/Prague, Hungary, Israel, and Cuba. The tours were built around visiting the most haunted locations in all those countries, and I personally hosted nearly all the trips.

A group of travelers joined me on a GHOSTour to England, 2009. Photo courtesy Kari Snider

Often, I'd have a respected tour guide joining me who was far more well-versed in the haunted locations and lore. One of the best personalities and most knowledgeable of my international co-hosts has been Richard Felix, who is best-known as one of the presenters of the long-running British television series *Most Haunted*. He hails from Derby,

Richard Felix guides our England GHOSTour in the town of York. Photo courtesy Kari Snider

England where he runs the haunted Derby Gaol (Jail) events. When he traveled to the U.S., I arranged for him to do a presentation at the library in Derby, Connecticut because he always wanted to visit one of the Derbys in New England.

We had some unforgettable and epic trips, and many travelers went from being regulars on the tours to being life-long friends.

Along the way, I expanded the GHOSTours to non-overseas locations such as New Orleans and San Francisco. We've also done a "Mayhem in Manhattan" weekend in New York as well as several getaways to Salem (MA) titled "Weekend of The Witch."

To me these tours were all part of my overall entertainment portfolio. These theme tours were, and always will be, a fun sideline for me, and an excuse to travel to different lands I may not have otherwise ever visited. I am a professional DJ/MC entertainer as my full-time vocation, but I do many other things. I've acted in films (yes, especially horror) and have done some television work and even theater. I produce Beatles and other music conventions and festivals (one of which was a non-music convention—ParaConn—a paranormal convention, but we'll get to that later), I book bands, and I host an interview show on a radio station. I once fronted a band as lead singer. I write songs. I wrote a play. I published and edited a music magazine for some 20 years. I wrote the online *National Horror Happenings* newsletter for years. I owned and was the founder of (and also acted in) a haunted attraction, and I published a horror book.

Why do I list all this? To illustrate that pretty much all of what I did (and do) always centered around entertaining, either revolving around music (mostly The Beatles and The Monkees) or the horror/monsters genre. Admittedly I love the scary stuff, and always tried to find ways to incorporate it into my productions. Having said that, I always viewed horror and monsters as being a separate, though arguably connected, entity (pardon the pun) from the paranormal world.

I became part of the paranormal community quite by accident (or was it divine intervention?). As the founder and original owner of Fright Haven, which is Connecticut's largest (and, may I add with possible bias, greatest) indoor haunted attraction, there I would greet visitors to the haunt and welcome them before letting them inside for the scares. I was "Cryptmaster Chucky," and, as an actor, humorist, and improvisationalist, I loved it. I would engage hundreds and sometimes thousands of people a night.

Nick Grossmann and Charles F. Rosenay!!! at the 2021 ParaConn

One evening, a rather cool-looking guest was in line ready to walk through. We exchanged banter for a few seconds, as I try to do with all the patrons, but whereas I do most of the talking and kibitzing, this particular visitor to the haunt made it a point to get in a few words edgewise. He told me that the building "was haunted." I laughed him off, saying "Of course it's haunted, we designed it that way." Fortunately, he didn't get insulted by what could have been perceived as me mocking him. He wasn't ruffled or offended. He insisted, "No, seriously, I sense that this place is truly haunted." Granted, we heard noises late at night when all the guests had left, but what building doesn't have its grunts and groans and audible idiosyncrasies? Before I waved him through the doors to enter, he went on to tell me that he was psychic and sensed something. He wanted to do a paranormal investigation of the venue, and I told him to get in touch with me. I never expected to hear from him again. He reached out immediately.

I don't know if it's true, but the plaza where the Fright Haven haunted attraction is housed was said to have been built above an original Native American burial ground! The guy who visited that night, Nick Grossmann, somehow sensed it! Mind you, I didn't believe him, but I liked his persona and confidence, and found him to be a unique character. Before too long, Nick suggested we have a "Ghost Lab" event at Fright Haven. I was up for anything that might potentially draw more attendees and publicity, so we booked an event we named "Ghost Lab: Proving the Paranormal" into Fright Haven. He had a team he called the "Ghost Storm," and this happening was to be a presentation totally separate from the haunted attraction's normally (if you can call all the jump-scares and animatronics "normal") staged scares.

The Fright Haven building was previously a cinema complex and then a huge Bally's gym, transformed by my "team of terror" or "fright family" into a seasonal haunted house. The facility had an upper deck area, which we rarely used. In this upstairs area, there was a completely mirrored room where we could squeeze in about 50 seated attendees.

We put out word about the event and it completely sold out. I welcomed the guests, as I always did, and then Nick and a few of his associates conducted the proceedings. The presentation ended with a "scrying session," and the people who attended had some incredible experiences. Non-believers were converted. Some told of us seeing their dead relatives appear. One skeptic swore he was staring in the mirror and all of the other 49 guests in the room that were there all disappeared! Another swore that he was the only one in the reflection while all the others in the room disappeared. Hmmm. All I knew was that everyone was pleased and entertained, and that was both my goal and job. The night was a success, and whether he actually "proved the paranormal" or not, Grossmann proved himself to me. If I was a non-believer in Nick being sincere or being capable of putting on a successful show before that night, he officially won me over. I was a fan, and soon a friend.

Grossmann and I became "para-partners." He was the real deal: a shaman, a clairvoyant, a psychic, an empath, a mystic, an exorcist, a medium, a cool guy. Above all, a friend. I am a producer, a promoter, and someone always open to new ways of entertaining folks. I soon came up with our title, "The Shaman and The Showman." It fits.

Together we began to co-host paranormal investigations throughout Connecticut, which were open to small groups of participants.

We hope you, the reader, are able to join us on future adventures (email CTParaConn@gmail.com to be added to our database).

I always heard about one place somewhere in the state called Dudleytown, but I never considered going there, let alone bringing groups there. Nick and I actually conducted several day hikes there (no, I wouldn't dare go alone at night), and we had great results. That expanded to other locations with me serving as not just a host, but actually one of the paranormal investigators. I've gotten to explore abandoned buildings and haunted residences, along with well-known and lesser-known haunted locations, some of which I'd heard of before, and others I'd never known existed.

I grew up knowing about and having interactions with the Warrens, undisputed paranormal legends in Connecticut (and the world, thanks to the *Conjuring* films). When magicians talk about magic, the name Houdini always comes up. When mentalists talk about their trade, The Amazing Kreskin is the first name that comes to mind (pun intended). When paranormal peeps talk about hauntings, the Warrens' name comes up. And deservedly so. I only have one story to share about them, and it's in this book.

Before meeting Nick, I had my own experiences, which I detail in this book, but I never thought I would be an actual paranormal investigator. I never considered myself to be a ghost-hunter. If I'm being perfectly honest, I still don't. Anyone who hunts for something wants to find it. *I don't!* If "it" wanted to be found that badly, it would find a way to be found… by someone else!

Along with taking small groups to reputedly haunted locations in the state, and, along with booking personal appearances and live, concert-like, interactive "Ghost Lab" shows into theaters and other venues, Nick and I produced Connecticut's first-ever Paranormal Convention in July of 2021, "ParaConn." He had planted the seed in my ear during the Covid months, and I jumped all over it. It wasn't a stretch for me to put the event together after having produced music-themed conventions since 1978. I'd also attended numerous horror fests and comic cons, so I knew the ingredients needed. With Grossmann's contacts and my production skills, we started promoting "ParaConn," which would be held at the Ansonia Armory in Ansonia, CT (an ominous building where we had also conducted a paranormal investigation). I expected a modest attendance, perhaps 200 or so people and a handful of vendors. We wound up booking 60 vendors and attracted over fifteen hundred attendees. Future ParaConns are in the works.

In 2021, I published *The Book of Top 10 Horror Lists*, wherein I collected and edited one hundred submissions from celebrities who gave me their top 10 lists of favorite horror or genre films and themes. I got the itch to write some more and decided to work on a personal book on the paranormal, centered around what Nick and I contend to be one of the most haunted states: Connecticut.

I was born and raised in The Bronx (no jokes about that being scarier than anything I could write about), but I've lived in Connecticut most of my life. It's a fair argument that Connecticut is an extremely haunted state.

Some people "believe in ghosts," while others mock the ones that believe. Most just don't know. Sort of like believing in a higher power. Some do, some don't, and some just don't know. I would venture to bet that even the most ardent non-believers, or skeptics, have had an unexplained occurrence—which may or may not have been supernatural. Ask just about anyone, and they will have a story to tell you, or an experience to share.

Is it otherworldly? Perhaps.

Can it be explained? Rarely.

Here, we have a collection of such stories.

If you're reading this book, you're either a friend of mine, or you already believe, or have possibly had your own experiences. In that case, none of the stories or recollections herein will surprise you. I'd love to hear *your* stories and experiences. Perhaps the next volume of *True Ghost Stories of Connecticut* can include what you've encountered. Email me at CTParaConn@gmail.com or phone (203) 795-4737. That's the same line to call if you're interested in any of our tours, conventions, investigations, or events.

You could also keep that number on file if you have a paranormal emergency. Seriously. Nick Grossmann is available to survey and analyze any supernatural scenarios, and he never charges for consultations, personal investigations, cleansings, or dire situations.

"Who you gonna call?"

There are other books, articles, and collections on the hauntings in Connecticut that have come before this one, and they're all worth reading. In no way is this a definitive collection, nor a guide to all the haunted locations in Connecticut, but perhaps there are a few new ones in here that you hadn't heard about, or some personal stories that will be new and of interest to you. Unlike past books, however, what you have here is a collection of stories and recollections from friends, colleagues, and professionals in the paranormal community. In that regard, you're getting a cross-section of articles/encounters, which I trust you'll find very interesting, informative and, in some cases, downright frightening.

Whether you are a believer or not, what's more important to me is that you enjoy the book. If you enjoy it, please write a positive review somewhere, get another copy for a friend as a gift, tell someone about it, or post about it on Facebook, Instagram, Twitter or anywhere online.

Fang you (thank you) for that, and Beast Wishes to you!

Cheers and Chills, "Cryptmaster Chucky" Charles F. Rosenay!!!

www.ParaConn.org
www.DracTours.com
www.LiverpoolTours
www.GHOSTour.com
www.SalemParaCon.org
www.ToursAndEvents.com
www.ParanormalConnecticut.com
www.BookOfTop10HorrorLists.com
www.BookOfTop10BeatlesLists.com

For information on Connecticut Paranormal Convention, visit www.ParaConn.org.

For info on Salem's Paranormal Convention, visit www.SalemParaCon.org.

For details on the Dracula Tour to Transylvania, go to www.DracTours.com.

For info on all of the GHOSTours, please check out www.ToursOfTerror.com.

Please buy my other (first) book on Amazon www.BookOfTop10HorrorLists.com

ENTER FREELY
AND OF YOUR OWN FREE WILL

I BID YOU WELCOME

CAROUSEL GARDENS

by Jimmy "Mr. Haunted" Petonito

On September 17, 1995, I was attending classes/meetings held by Ed and Lorraine Warren for the New England Society for Psychic Research. The meetings were held on Mondays at the Warrens' home in Monroe, Connecticut. Sometimes the meetings would be instructional, other times we talked about new or ongoing cases we were working on. One evening Lorraine mentioned that there was a restaurant that was possibly haunted, and the owner wanted us to check it out. When asked

Carousel Gardens exterior photo by Jimmy Petonito

who would like to go, another investigator, Dave, and I raised our hands. Lorraine gave us directions. The restaurant was called Carousel Gardens in Seymour, Connecticut (in 2009, the building became a beauty school).

We arrived at around 7 PM and were greeted by the owners, Paul and Debbie Schiarffa. The building was a huge, blue Victorian mansion with white trim. It was covered in tiny white lights and certainly didn't look haunted. Paul told us a little of the home's history and gave us a tour. We learned that before it was a restaurant, it was a 20-room mansion formerly owned by William Wooster and home to the Wooster family.

William Wooster was a Civil War soldier who moved to Seymour in 1878 with his wife and six children. Wooster is considered to be the founder of Seymour. He founded a bank, a water company, a manufacturing company, and was heavily involved with the schools and church in town. The last surviving family member and the last to live in the house was Ruth. She seemed to be the spirit (amongst others) most seen and heard.

As we entered the busy restaurant, the first thing we noticed were actual flying horses from old amusement parks throughout the dining area. It was brightly lit, with music playing over the sound system. Paul started telling us the stories of Ruth still roaming the mansion and sometimes interacting with patrons and employees. Many nights it was customary for the employees to hang around a little bit after the restaurant closed and have a couple drinks and listen to some music. Apparently, Ruth didn't like this, and she wanted quiet after the restaurant was closed. One night, a few lingering employees all witnessed an apparition of a woman walking by the hallway next to the bar area where they were

Jimmy Petonito with The Warrens. Photos courtesy of Jimmy Petonito

sitting. They saw her put her finger to her mouth as if to say "Shhh." On other occasions she could be heard humming or singing. Ruth would turn the lights on and off or turn the music off, and they understood this was their cue to pack up and go home. And they would leave.

On one particular night, a bartender told us she was working the bar, standing behind the cash register talking to one of the patrons, when the cash register levitated into the air at least six inches before it dropped onto the floor and smashed in front of multiple witnesses. Numerous times, members of the wait staff would hear a glass smash onto the kitchen floor but when they went to clean it up, there would be no glass to be found.

The restaurant was a hot spot for psychic "ghost" photographs. I captured a few strange images on film the first visit and gave them to Paul. Paul started a photographic Rolodex which he kept on a small table by the front door, so when people came in they could look through the ghost pictures that people captured at the place.

After our initial investigation, we had multiple investigations thereafter, as the owners were very accommodating. One moment stuck out from the rest.

On October 30, 1995, Connecticut country radio station WWYZ joined up with our group for an overnight Halloween broadcast. After the restaurant closed for the evening, Ed and Lorraine, a few of us investigators, a few employees, and the radio station crew remained. John Garabo, the DJ of their popular morning show, was doing the overnight shift for this special Halloween broadcast.

I was excited. We've finally hit the big time! An actual overnight with a popular radio show live on air! They would go about their regular broadcast playing songs, every so often they would check with the investigators for updates.

We had a "psychomanteum" set up in one of the closets off the main dining area. A psychomanteum is a dimly lit enclosed area with only a mirror on the wall. The belief is that spirits can manifest in the mirror using this method. We lined the closet with black trash bags, hung a mirror on the wall, and put a small, red, light bulb under the mirror, like a Christmas tree bulb. It served as the only light source when the door was closed. A small chair was placed inside, with the

Lorraine Warren inside Carousel Gardens. Photo by Jimmy Petonito

idea being someone would sit in the chair and stare into the mirror with only that small light as illumination.

People would get "locked in" the psychomanteum for 20 minutes at a time. A few ran out screaming and left the premises, so I never knew what they saw. I recall one gentleman burst out of the room almost crying, saying he saw all these scary animal-looking creatures coming at him from inside the mirror. I sat in the room; sadly (but maybe gladly) I saw and heard nothing.

Before going live on the air some of us had been sitting in the dining area just talking. All the tables were set up so they'd be ready for the next day. DJ John Garabo confessed to us that he didn't really believe in "this stuff" but that it would make for a fun Halloween show. The second he finished that sentence a glass a few tables away from us "exploded." I interviewed him afterwards and this was his exact quote as he pointed across the room: "A glass just exploded across the way at about ten of ten tonight. We were just sitting here talking and heard this loud crashing sound like someone smashed a glass onto concrete. We looked around, there was no one near this table and this glass just exploded into a million pieces." I was thinking maybe he does believe in "this stuff" now.

Sadly, John Garabo passed away March 16, 2012, in his sleep at the age of 46. He was on the air for 25 years in radio. Hopefully you have all the answers now. RIP John.

Jimmy Petonito began taking photos in haunted cemeteries in the late eighties. In 1991 he shared his findings with Ed and Lorraine Warren. He was invited to be a member of the New England Society for Psychic Research and was trained by —and worked alongside—the Warrens. He has appeared on the TV shows "Sightings," "Unsolved Mysteries," and ABC's "Primetime Live." Jimmy is also featured in the documentary "Hostage to the Devil" and the shock doc "Devils Road." He has assisted in 50 exorcisms and for ten years taught a ghost hunting class at a local high school where he earned the nickname "Mr. Haunted." He has also co-authored the book "Phantom Messages" with Bill Hall and hosts the radio show "The Haunted Chronicles."

THE CHRIS MARK CASTLE OF WOODSTOCK

by Christine and Daniel Peer

Many know of the breathtaking Chris Mark Castle in Woodstock, Connecticut. What many don't know is that a half-mile down the road from the castle sits the original farmhouse to the property, also owned by Christopher Mark. The farmhouse dates back to the pre-Revolutionary War and holds many secrets within its walls. Over the years it's had a few different owners and at one point was a tavern. The house sat vacant for quite a few years in between each owner to the point of being restored more than once. Chris has done an amazing job restoring this beautiful home and saving all the original fireplaces within the rooms. For some time, the home was lived in by caretakers of his property, yet they would always disappear in the middle of night or refuse to stay in the house, opting instead to stay in the attic above the barn which has been converted to living quarters. They complained of hearing footsteps, seeing shadows, etc., that scared them to be in the house.

Chris Mark Castle in Woodstock, Connecticut

So once again, the home is empty. In hopes of turning this beautiful historic house into a B&B, Chris Mark reached out to The Connecticut Paranormal Research Team to investigate the claims of activity within the home.

The team arrived on Friday, May 15, 2021, and immediately started unloading the vehicles and setting up equipment. They spent a good two hours wiring cameras to their DVR system and preparing the night's investigation. Working alongside the team was Gregory Harris, who helped film the team throughout the night.

While setting up equipment, team director Christine Peer, along with investigator Christopher Jodoin, headed up to the third-floor bedroom with equipment. While up there the ceiling fan immediately turned on by itself, even though neither had flipped any switches.

At that point, they waited for it to stop and turned on every light switch up there to try to get it to happen again. They even placed a motion detector on it, but the entire evening it never turned a blade. The actions of the fan coming on by itself could not be explained.

The Mark farmhouse

The team did a complete EMF sweep of the entire location looking to see if there was an electrical or man-made electromagnetic field leaking into the property causing the possible paranormal feelings. Tests proved the location to be completely well grounded. While the DVR recorded all evening into the morning hours, the team tried several different experiments to communicate with whatever was there.

At one point in the evening, a new recruit named Charlie joined the team on his first investigation and a sensory deprivation experiment was tried on him. He was blindfolded and given noise-canceling headphones while listening to white noise so he could not hear anyone. He was placed in one of the second-floor bedrooms alone with just Greg filming him along with a DVR camera. From the living room the team would ask questions and see if Charlie would respond with any answers that he heard come through the white noise. Charlie said he sensed a man in the room and kept hearing a faint piano playing in the background. Oddly, none of that audio was captured on the DVR but it was an experience that Charlie will not forget.

On two different occasions downstairs in the living room, the team heard the sound of the porch door opening. Despite staring at it and anticipating someone entering the room, the door never opened. The door opened by team members to see if it was the same sound heard and it was. No one was outside on the porch. Throughout the evening, there were sounds of footsteps of someone walking upstairs, yet everyone from the team was all in the living room. Eric Quinn, Chris Jodoin, and Charlie went to the third floor for an EVP session to capture electronic voice phenomenon while also using a trigger object of a Raggedy Ann doll that had a built-in K2 meter in case it was the spirit of a child. They did get some spikes with the doll but were unsuccessful in getting any EVPs. The team then decided to try using the Kinect SLS camera system, which maps out the room and shows a skeletal figure of people or spirits in the room.

Daniel Peer went through the entire house to be sure the system was running properly. At one point he was in the main entrance of the house while the rest of the team was in the attic, and the DVR camera in the back dining room caught a shadow figure going up the staircase. While setting up earlier in the evening, the team thought they saw someone go upstairs yet no one had.

Inside the farmhouse

Close to midnight, Dan and Christine were getting spikes on the K2 meters in the upstairs bedroom. The remainder of the team was monitoring the DVR. A lot of commotion was going on downstairs, to what appeared on the DVR as an apparition moving across another bedroom on the second floor above the porch. After analyzing over and over, as it happened a couple of times, the team unfortunately, debunked the apparition. It was a car that had gone by, and the headlights had reflected through the window. This would have been a great piece of evidence, but it had to be ruled out.

Regardless of missing that footage, between the personal experiences and capturing the shadow figure and unexplained movement on the third floor, the home was in fact haunted.

The spirits there are nothing of a negative nature and are just going about their business as if it was still back in the time frame they lived there.

The rumors of the property include a 14-year-old girl who was sick and disappeared. To this day she has never been found. There is also the legend of the two men that got into a sword fight over a barmaid that they would visit when it was a tavern, and they both died within the building.

No hard evidence of these occurrences actually taking place in this location was unearthed, but the walls within this home are holding back many secrets from over the decades that are just waiting to be told.

Whenever 450 Brickyard Road in Woodstock opens its doors as a bed and breakfast, CTPRT will definitely be back to conduct more investigations. Book a night and hopefully you too will experience what these walls may tell.

Who knows, maybe we'll be there to join you. To follow us on future investigations, visit website: www.connecticutparanormal.com

The Connecticut Paranormal Research Team was established in 2000 and is based out of Northeastern Connecticut. CPRT is a volunteer research group headed by Christine and Daniel Peer. The goal of the organization is to investigate and document paranormal phenomena to determine whether a residence and/or an establishment is, in fact, haunted. They conduct their investigation using a scientific approach. By using equipment to detect, communicate with, and capture evidence of paranormal activity, they also try to find natural causes for what may be perceived as paranormal activity, before jumping to the conclusion that a place is haunted.

Christine Peer has been the director of the team for the last 22 years, with her history in the field dating back 43 years. She has helped hundreds of families across the East Coast and will continue to dedicate her life in the field.

Daniel Peer joined the team 10 years ago and has always had an interest in the paranormal. He is the mad scientist of the team when it comes to building equipment and broadcasting cases.

Besides investigations, the team has participated in many presentations and expos, while appearing on many internet/radio stations, TV broadcasts, and motion pictures; as well as producing their own broadcasted and pre-recorded internet cases.

Photos Courtesy of The Paranormal Couple

DARK SIEGE: A CONNECTICUT FAMILY'S NIGHTMARE

by Jason McLeod

The most fascinating and terrifying case I have ever personally investigated occurred in 1993 in Monroe, Connecticut, just days before Halloween. It began wi-h a chance drive by of one of the most haunted cemeteries in New England, the infamous Union Cemetery in Easton. Linda McLaughlin and her six-year-old daughter Kelly were passing slowly by the rusted wrought iron gates in a torrential downpour and Kelly spotted a jet-black shape in the form of a man, walking through the gravestones, through the gates, and right up toward the car before her astonished eyes. As Kelly turned her head slowly toward the back window of the station wagon, the monster, for it certainly had to be a monster, kept disappearing and reappearing three feet closer until he was seen pressing his spectral hands up against the glass of the window causing Kelly to scream so loud, her mother cut the wheel causing the car to spin out on the slick fallen leaves lining the road.

The spirit followed them home and, of course, no one believed Kelly when she did her best to try and explain the scary scene as it unfolded earlier.

The next afternoon when Kelly's 16-year-old brother Tyler and his two best friends came home after school, they experienced the same black form, spotting it walking the outside perimeter of the property. When they rushed outside to confront the stranger, he vanished before their eyes and when the teens gazed back at the back of the house, they saw the sliding glass door close, by itself.

Upon re-entering the house, they witnessed physical objects moving by themselves and liquor bottles smashing behind the bar, which was enough for them to run right back out of the house through the garage. They made the worst mistake of their young lives by deciding to go to the Trumbull Mall to purchase a Ouija board so they could try to get some form of communication going.

Once they returned to the house, they issued all the wrong challenges and unleashed a campaign of terror the likes they nor I have never before experienced first-hand when not one but eight inhuman, diabolical spirits infested the house to oppress everyone inside when they were the most vulnerable in an effort to possess them.

This case, which became known as *Dark Siege: A Connecticut Family's Nightmare* was recreated in a horror fiction format with a cinematic writing style readers find impossible to put down and challenging to read at night. Readers feel like they are right there, experiencing the blinding terror the family and their friends endure in each captivating chapter.

Jason McLeod is a paranormal investigator, spiritualist, demonologist, and intuitive empath born, raised, and based in Connecticut, where he has spent the last 32 years helping individuals and families deal with the discarnate human spirits who linger in their lives, and the inhuman spirits who seek to ruin them. His training and experience began in 1990 under none other than the late, legendary Ed and Lorraine Warren while he was a student attending classes at both the NESPR (New England Society for Psychic Research) and SHU (Sacred Heart University) in Fairfield, Connecticut. There, he wrote the column 'Hauntings' for the SHU Spectrum newspaper, chronicling the astounding cases they were investigating together. Soon after, he was spirited away to Washington State to pursue his Creative Writing degree at Eastern Washington University.

The Warrens asked McLeod to investigate a serious case in nearby Rathdrum, Idaho on their behalf. After the case had been successfully resolved, McLeod formed the Northwest Society for Paranormal Research and taught weekly classes on campus to intrigued students and the general populace.

McLeod graduated with a BA in Letters and Social Sciences / English-Creative Writing and with it, a unique, captivating, cinematic writing style he would utilize years later that would enable him to recreate his most astounding cases with an immersive and captivating quality that would make readers feel as if they themselves were experiencing everything that happened firsthand.

Upon returning to Connecticut in 1993, McLeod became embroiled in the most terrifying case of Demonic Infestation, Oppression, Possession, and Exorcism he had ever experienced to date. He revealed the startling details in 2012 via his debut self-published novel titled "Dark Siege: A Connecticut Family's Nightmare." He then began lecturing at Paranormal Conventions and Spirituality Expositions nationwide before releasing the sequel, "Dark Siege: The Nightmare Returns" in 2014. McLeod is currently writing "Dark Siege: The Demon of Daybreak Farm," detailing a terrifying case he investigated with the Warrens in Vermont in 1990. Following that, he plans to release "Dark Siege: Rage in Rathdrum," which will recreate the case he investigated on the Warrens' behalf in Rathdrum, Idaho in 1991.

McLeod conducts engaging presentations and lectures on the subjects of spirituality, consciousness, quantum physics, metaphysics, paranormal investigation, and demonology on radio blog broadcasts, paranormal conventions, and spirituality expositions throughout the country.

Jason resides in Southbury, Connecticut and spends time in Austin, Texas, where he utilizes his creativity as co-songwriter, lyricist, and lead vocalist in the Progressive Metal band he co-founded called Shadow Ministry. The web page is www.shadowministryband.com.

He may be reached by email at mcleodmetaphysics@protonmail.com. For more on the Dark Siege Series visit www.darksiege.com.

Jason McLeod and Lorraine Warren in her kitchen, Spring 2016.
Photo courtesy Jason McLeod

DERBY'S STERLING OPERA HOUSE

by Rich DiCarlo

Before I get into telling you about this place, I'd like to tell you a bit about my experience in the field.

I have been interested in the paranormal since my first experiences with a "shadow" man entity that I encountered on a regular basis, so much so that I actually became accustomed to its appearances. Now don't get me wrong, I was terrified for years. Fifty-something years later, it has become so much like seeing a bright colored cardinal in the backyard. I stop and look, and admire it, and then go about my day.

Though I have been blessed with great experiences, almost to the level of "fantastical," I am not an expert of the paranormal, nor do I believe there are any so-called "experts" on the subject. Just those with a certain level of "experience." Nobody truly knows what we are dealing with. Nobody has all the answers. In my book, a five-year-old who saw the "Boogeyman" in his bedroom, in the middle of the night, is more of an expert than many so-called 'seasoned' investigators. An open mind, rationality, and some skepticisms are required to explain many situations that we encounter. I currently own and I also grew up in a house that was not necessarily 'haunted.' We were able to live in it, along with whatever entity or power that shared the dwelling with us. I refer to it as being "active." I consider The Sterling Opera House to be in the same vein.

I have led many paranormal explorations, been an active member of several investigative groups, spoken publicly on the subject, and appeared in the newspapers and on the local news, as well as several popular television programs such as *Ghost Hunters*, *Destination Fear*, etc.

Halloween in 2013 was when I became personally connected to the Sterling Opera House in Derby, Connecticut. The place was built in 1889 by Charles Sterling, owner of the Sterling Piano factory, a once thriving industrial entity back in the day. Unfortunately, Charles never saw its completion. The facility was quite unusual for its time because it was not only a theater but a multi-function building. Unlike the title suggests, an "Opera House" was a generic term for theaters such as this. The stage was actually too small for operatic performances, so its theater served as a vaudeville and burlesque-type venue. Movie theaters were not in existence at that time, yet its multi—functionality was

Inside Sterling Opera House. Photo courtesy Rich DiCarlo

quite novel for its time. The majestic structure served as (on the ground floor) Derby City Hall, The Basset Fire House, and even The Police Department, complete with jail cells. The theater itself occupied the second and third floors.

Researching the history of the building, it read like a who's who of performers that walked through the doors. The same performers traveled by train throughout the country and appeared in practically every town on the circuit. So if your town had a train station, you had a Hotel and an Opera House…just like Derby.

There is no record of any person having ever died in the place. There was, however, a person who got struck by lightning through an open window. There used to be a funeral parlor, where the courthouse now stands next door and the Hotel Clark, across the alley that was once Fourth Street. On the other side, there was an accidental death. It is important to make this clear, as many so-called psychics/sensitives came forward to say the place is full of many tragic deaths. Historic records say otherwise. I don't want to sensationalize the place and I will defend its reputation.

Famed magician, illusionist, and spiritualist Harry Houdini was a regular at this venue. Like many other stages, the stages were altered with trap doors to accommodate the illusions in his act. As history/lore indicated, Houdini claimed that he would prove that there was an afterlife by appearing via séance, or whatever means of conveyance, on Halloween night. This would explain my introduction to the structure. I was a member of the Derby Cultural Commission, and, along with a group of folks interested in the subject, we would be conducting a Halloween Night session to contact Mr. Houdini. I was 100% aware of the fact that we were never going to contact him, based on the countless others throughout the world who attempted to do the same thing at the same time. What on earth would make "Derby" be his place of choice to return from the dead?

Nevertheless, the frivolous attempt was still made. The building had no electricity or heat. It was undergoing renovation on the outer structure and was basically a vacant shell of a building. Being cold, bored, and quite tired of the repetitive calling out to Harry, I decided to take a walk around the building to explore the place with camera in hand. It was obviously dark, but the lights from the streets eerily illuminated the wide staircases at the front of the building. Now, being the experienced person that I was, I had an open mind while wandering the place, knowing full well about light and shadow play, matrixing and whatever the mind/imagination can throw at you. I stopped to peer at the city through the large ornate spider web-shaped window, in the tower part of the staircase, at the left side of the building. In my peripheral vision there appeared to be movement in the shadows at the balcony above my head. My first thought was that it was some creature like a raccoon or a large rat.

I nonchalantly turned my head towards the noise and saw what appeared to be a dark mass, darker than the darkness that engulfed the upper area. It took me a moment to realize that I had a camera in hand and snapped a photograph. I later examined the photo on my computer and saw what appeared to be dark shadow figures at the top of the balcony.

I kept my photographs secret for a while until the famed and respected historian, Richard Felix, author of the book *What is a Ghost?*, and perhaps best known as one of the hosts of the British television series *Most Haunted*, came to Derby with his wife for a presentation at the local library. Coincidentally, the author of this book, Charles F. Rosenay!!!, was a close friend of Richard Felix, and the two of them hosted many ghost-themed group tours to haunted locations in the U.K. Because Richard is from Derby in Great Britain, he asked Charles to arrange a visit to a Derby city in the U.S.

After his library appearance, the Mayor of Derby hosted Mr. Felix for a private walk-through of the Opera House. We had several experiences there, and he looked at my evidence, confirming that what I had captured on the camera appeared to be of paranormal origin. I was very intrigued and got permission to further investigate. This was the beginning of a seven-year investigation that was comprised of about 40 or so teams from all over the country.

Along with many groups, I took countless photographs and recordings of the activities here and consider most of them to be "Class A" evidence. Though there are countless grunts and perceived EVPs; for the most part if you heard a person say "hello" or "leave," it was one of many times. It was that kind of a place. The entities, aside from one, are peaceful. Many visitors have been physically slapped and scratched when not heeding warnings. I can write an entire book on the Opera House but for the sake of sanity, will focus on a few main incidents.

Over the years, through many reliable "sensitives" and recording devices, we have concluded that there are eighteen entities inhabiting the place. Several are intelligent and are identifiable by name and can sometimes identify us by name. Contrary to all those television shows that have everything happen at midnight or 3 AM, the most incredible stuff has occurred in the afternoon and early evening, when the place probably would have been active back in the day.

On October 30, 2014, I entered the Opera House with a group of local reporters to do a Halloween article of the place. Upon entering the building, we all heard the voice of a child say "Hi." The stairs had areas of such extreme cold that you could see your breath in front of you. One area had us spellbound for over forty-five minutes. Our team experienced a blue ball of light, about the size of a softball, float down the stairs and stop in front of us before it would disappear. This activity repeated itself as we all attempted to figure out what was occurring. It was not on the wall, nor did it refract as a flashlight was shining on the steps. It was truly a free-floating transparent ball of blue light. After a while, this light would seemingly get accustomed to us being present and we were allowed to get closer and closer until I was able to sit on the steps and have it stop next to me. It was more fascinating than frightening and I was able to pass my hand underneath it and noticed that this ball of light did not illuminate my hand nor the step below. It was silent and very cold and broke up into little specks if I passed my hand through it. Then it would come down the steps and pretty much do the same thing over and over. The repetition, though quite fascinating, was getting to be a bit much—like a puppy wanting constant attention. It was getting late, and we moved away from the landing. The ball came down again and was able to descend the entire staircase and disappear into the doorway of the small ticket window at the bottom of the steps. We continued for about twenty minutes, and although the ball of light did not return that night, it was a frequent activity throughout the years, being seen throughout the theater area.

The most common entity at the Derby Opera House was what we call the "Green Lady." She goes by the name of "Hetty," and was apparently from Brooklyn, New York. She used to be the person in charge of the dancers who performed on the stage. I had the honor to speak to one of the former dancers, back in the late 1930s. Mary, a woman in her early 90s, confirmed the name and the personality behind the popular entity. Practically every time you walked in the door, she was present. She was regularly recorded greeting us and telling where you cannot go. She has shown us very interesting spots, such as the "kissing wall" where the girls, adorned with heavy lipstick, would lie on their backs, and kiss the lower wall in the so-called "green room" behind the stage. I guess this was in the same manner of kissing the Blarney Stone in Ireland for good luck. Hetty would accompany you throughout the night if she did not greet you at the door. Though it was rare to see her, she would appear as a greenish light from under the stage, hence the name "Green Lady." There are several photographs of her in various stages of "visuality." One group has an unbelievable photograph of her, wearing a teal greenish dress, as a full-bodied apparition. I was present at the moment of the astounding capture, right next to the photographer and

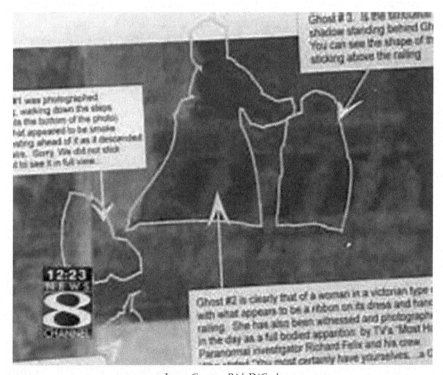

Image Courtesy Rich DiCarlo

I honestly did not see a thing! Hetty was a powerful entity and would physically strike a person who did not heed a warning. We have many recordings of her telling an investigator, "It's not safe for us there," then slapping or unintentionally scratching (it was meant to be a slap on the back of their neck, the common strike area for her) the person who disobeyed the message. She would often leave a red handprint.

The second most common—and the most fascinating of anything I have ever encountered here—is my pal "Andy." Over the years, I established an interdimensional bond (or whatever it is) with him.

This entity was most playful and active between 3pm and 8pm. I have never experienced him outside of this time though, surprisingly, he may have said something (unintelligible) on the "Ghost Hunters" episode. I had told them that the place was regularly active in the afternoons, but they went in at midnight. Their loss!

Like Hetty, Andy is a particularly strong presence with the ability to verbally communicate (you can actually hear him talk). He can move objects and he was captured a few times on camera and video. I have no record of his history outside of knowing that there were kids living in the house that once presided at the site of the Opera House. There is no historic connection to the place. Andy's presence, though strong, for some reason, can only travel through certain parts of the building. The name "Andy" was the result of several recorded answers to that question. The entity would get abrupt (bang or knock something) if you called it "Andrew."

My first experience with the entity goes back to an investigation when an audible "Help me" alerted us to the presence of the entity. In later investigations, we began to place toys (little cars and horses) here and there throughout the building and found them to be moved around the building. It was a ball used in an investigation that really got things started. One evening I headed a group of investigators that placed a ball at the top of the staircase (where the aforementioned blue light appeared). We sat for three hours, with cameras and recorders going, asking for Andy to move the ball, but to no avail. The crew took a break and gathered in the back of the theater area. For the sake of safety, I took the ball off the top of the steps and while the camera was going, I playfully said, "Hey kid, how hard was it to move the damn ball?" while making "wooing sounds" and making believe the ball was floating towards the camera lens. I joined the others in the back of the theater and relocated the ball at the base of some chairs in the corner. A second after I released my hand from the ball it shot across the room and violently ricocheted off the wall back at me. I screamed and ran out of the building. I don't think my feet even touched the floor. I regained my composure and went back inside. I was ridiculed, but they all saw that I was nowhere near the ball after it was "kicked."

The next night we noticed that the ball was nowhere in the building! The next week we set up a camera in a lower hallway of City Hall and left it rolling. Upon reviewing the recording, we heard our "Andy" taunting me through a song-like banter, accompanied by a deeper voice that repeated the song. "Hey you, hey you! My name is Andy, and I got my ba…aaa…all." This is all online. You can't make this kind of stuff up.

Andy is responsible for attracting the television crews to the location. It was on a Sunday morning when the producers from a certain program had wanted to investigate our paranormal activity claims. They were a husband-and-wife team, a psychic and cameraman with an assistant who manned the monitors and technological stuff. They were rather cavalier about the situation, planning on wrangling up the spirits and parading them down to the stage area. Perceiving the possibility of a long, wasted day in the theater, I sat myself down on the stage with the assistant as the couple climbed the narrow side stairway that passed from the stage through all the levels of the theater to the upper balcony. They stopped at the top of the balcony, in front of a bank of chairs that were reserved for the lower-class patrons (what we consider the "nose-bleed seats" in a stadium). I noticed that they were situated in one seat for quite some time when I asked, "Is there something wrong?" The woman replied that there was a little boy there. That sparked my interest and I wandered up to join them. She told me that he had his hand on her knee and was communicating with her. The area was noticeably very much colder over the seat. The husband told me to check out what he had on the viewfinder monitor. I witnessed what appeared to be a dancing little light, resembling a piece of tinsel being dangled. I peered at the seat and saw nothing there, and then back at the camera's view monitor, and then again at the seat, where there was nothing. The woman then called him "Andrew," and everything stopped.

She then said that he did not like to be called "Andrew" and referred to him as Andy along with an "it's Rich"—referring to my presence. She began to communicate back and forth. There was nothing audible to the human ear but the information she was divulging seemed to match up with others' notes of past investigations. I had never divulged the nitty gritty bits of the many previous investigations, in fear of people reading or hearing of them and then creating a false impression of what goes on there... just to get their 15 minutes of fame.

    I was still very skeptical as to what was actually happening and continually watched them like a hawk. She asked Andy a question and she said he touched her arm. I noticed the little camera display had stopped and the camera light shut off at the same time as the other pieces of equipment. I knew this from the assistant giving a holler that it went dead on her end. A small handheld camcorder was still in operation and captured what was one of the most stunning things that I have ever witnessed. The best way to describe it was that it was like one of those cheap toy wax slates with the gray plastic sheet that you would write on with a little plastic stylus. You draw an image and lift the sheet and the image would erase. It looked like that, but in reverse, with the image of a small child-sized hand forming in the thick blanket of dust that coated the seats, right in front of our very eyes! Everyone gasped in amazement. It was both terrifying and amazing at the same time. The image was caught on video, and they shared it with producers of the *Ghost Hunters* television program, who were there within a matter of days. Unfortunately, to get the jump on the other shows, they hurriedly jammed it into the season that was already shot, and disappointedly lumped it together with a lesser investigation ("A Soldier's Story"). It should have been a stand-alone episode. What was included in the show and what occurred...that's a story for another day. It truly was an amazing place with incredible encounters and activity.

    I had the honor of having access and getting to experience the activity for just about every weekend for several years. We had folks who had been in there for years and never saw a thing and others who experienced stuff that was out of this world. From what I've discovered, you just can't walk into a place and see or experience a ghost. Like a radio station, you can't hear the music if you have the radio turned off or set to the wrong station. You'd have to be tuned in.

Richard "ChiD" DiCarlo is an Artist/Cartoonist originating from New York City. He resides in Derby, Connecticut with his wife Wendy and two children, Alexandra and Maxwell, two dogs and a cat, and a ghost named "Patrick." He has appeared on several Paranormal Investigative programs such as Ghost Hunters *and* Destination Fear. *He is no stranger to paranormal activity having a grandfather who was a prominent seer, having*  *served as a spiritual advisor in certain New York circles in the 1930s and '40s and having grown up in an affected household.*

DERBY'S STERLING OPERA HOUSE: MORE PROOF OF THE PARANORMAL

by Margaret Scholz

Over the years, I have had the pleasure of investigating Derby, Connecticut's Sterling Opera House at least three times. Twice I was a member of a paranormal group. The other time I was the guest paranormal investigator on a *Ghosts of Derby* tour.

During my first visit, several weird and unexplainable things occurred. I came in the middle of summer with a paranormal group that I was a part of at the time, and there were about four or five of us investigating this night.

We started on the main floor and stage area. While the others were taking pictures from the main floor, I decided to go up onto the stage. I went to the middle of the stage, and I don't know why, but I did what I have always wanted to do on a stage: I spread out my arms and shouted: "All actors to your positions! The show must go on!"

I then stood there for a little while, and after a few minutes, I started to feel cold spots around me where I was standing on the stage. It felt like people were zooming by me. I can envision the skeptics saying, "Oh, the air conditioning was on," or "Oh, there were open windows," or "Oh, it was a cold night outside." Skeptics begin every sentence with the word "oh." Nope, there was no air conditioning in the building, nor were there any open windows, and it was the middle of summer and very warm that night.

I told the others what I was feeling, and asked them to take pictures. Unfortunately, nothing came out in the pics. After a while, we broke up into groups of two and went to different levels and areas in the building.

An investigator and I went to the second level seating. When we came up to the area from the left side stairway, I placed a voice recorder that I had brought along with me onto the arm of a seat on that level and left it there running. To ensure that it wouldn't fall, I placed it facing the same way as the arm of the seat. We then left the area to investigate the other side of the second level.

We walked over to the other side of the second level and set up a video camera and some toys as trigger objects. We had been told that one of the ghosts was said to be a child and so we brought the toys for him to play with.

We spent a couple of hours asking the child to come play with us, move the toys, etc. Nothing happened for us until we had turned off the video and we were collecting the toys. Each group was given a walkie talkie in case something happened and we had to get in touch with each other. Through the walkie talkie, we heard a child's voice asking "Who are you?" Shocked by this, we looked at each other and said, basically at the same time, "Did you hear that?" I then turned to the other investigators who were on the stage area and asked if they had heard a child's voice come through the walkie talkie. They did not.

Margaret Scholz

We then went back to pick up the voice recorder that I'd left on the seat arm. When we reached the chair, I noticed that the recorder was not in the same position as I had left it.

It had rotated about a quarter of a turn on the arm.

Thinking it may have moved when we walked away, we placed it back in the position I had originally put it in and tried walking, stomping, and jumping up and down to see if it would change position, but not once did it move.

Not finding a logical reason for the movement, I had to believe that "someone" else had moved it. Perhaps it was the child who spoke to us through the walkie talkie?

We joined the other group, and one of the other investigator's walkie talkie started making weird static noises. I told him that since I had mine and we were all together, he could just turn his walkie talkie off, and he did. We then started up the stairs to the cupola. He had just gotten to the top of the stairs, when the walkie talkie that he had turned off began to make noises again. No one was near him, and both of his hands were on the stair railings.

After that we visited the other areas of the opera house including the area under the stage and the jail cells. Nothing else happened, it just seemed to go quiet after that. We came back again, with some experiments to try. However, it was a very quiet visit.

In 2018, I was asked to be a guest paranormal investigator in the opera house during a ghost tour of Derby that year. I was in the opera house with all of the equipment I normally used on investigations. I was prepared to tell the guests about my experiences in the building, and then they would ask questions about my equipment, and try it all out if they wanted to.

Before the first guests arrived, I had decided to put a video camera on the stage and film a ball and another toy as trigger objects. I placed them within my arm's reach on the stage and went to finish setting up before any of the people arrived. I had also decided to put an EMF meter, known as a "boo bear," on a seat across from where my table was.

During the evening, I noticed that the bear kept lighting up. I checked to make sure it wasn't malfunctioning or near anything that would make it go off. Every time I—or someone else—approached, the bear would stop lighting up. When we walked away, it would light up again. I figured it might be the child spirit playing with it so I let him enjoy himself.

Another interesting thing happened when a young woman came in with her camera. It was a professional camera with a long lens attached, and it had to have cost a pretty penny. She started to take photos of the inside of the building, but for some reason her camera wouldn't work. We informed her that one of the stories of the opera house is that "someone" won't let people take pictures unless they ask permission first. So we asked politely and after that her camera worked fine.

Finally, as the evening was winding down and we started to pack up, I went to retrieve my video camera and toys off the stage. When I reached the stage, I was able to grab my video camera, but was unable to reach the toys. They had somehow moved farther onto the stage out of reach. When I got home, I checked the camera, but whatever happened occurred after the camera ended its recording.

The opera house is a very cool and interesting place for both its history and hauntings.

I hope I can get back in there again in the future.

DOWN IN THE VALLEY: BEYOND THE OPERA HOUSES

by Michael James Mascolo

It's funny to think about the paranormal: spirits, specters, things that may go bump in the night. The phenomenon of it all is that hopefully we can catch a glimpse of some spirit searching for the afterlife. Or maybe a ghostly image that can't find his way to the other side. This is a segue to several small stories related to my experiences growing in Derby, Connecticut.

My father owned several properties on Elizabeth Street, including the James Furniture Company and the Commodore Hull Theatre building. The theater was built in 1927 as a vaudeville theater. Just a few doors down stood, and is still standing, the Sterling Opera House. Around this same time, my uncle purchased the Ansonia Opera House.

The James Furniture Building

Let's start with the James Furniture building. Before its name change in the early sixties, it was known as Lee Brothers Furniture. The Lee brothers came from England and became distributors of fine furni-

From the Collection of Michael James Mascolo

ture. The building was sold to my family in the early '60s. James Furniture was a five-story building with a five-story warehouse. It basically still stands where Raro's Motor Car Garage is today.

When you walked in the lobby—or main floor—of the furniture store there was an old-fashioned elevator to your right, with a sliding gate to engage. There was also a grand staircase that made the main floor very Victorian looking. There were always rumors of some kind of haunting that happened on the fourth or fifth floors. At this point, being 10-11 years old, I never saw anything in this particular building. That is, until one afternoon when my father's partner walked up the five floors instead of taking the elevator. He had been accompanying a family buying furniture. As he was writing their order up, he sat down on one of the chairs and passed away right then and there of a heart attack. From this point on, everybody was literally spooked in the building. There were 25 employees, and not one wanted to go to the fourth or fifth floor, insisting that they heard strange noises and saw weird things. Usually, they heard someone talking on those floors, but it was unrecognizable. Other odd and unexplained things would happen, including tables and chairs being turned upside down.

Derby Demolition: The James Building comes down.
From the Collection of Michael James Mascolo

Perhaps scariest would be the elevator turning itself on and off every morning. They would have to walk up to bring it back to the main floor. My father, who did not believe in any of this at all, decided to throw the switches to turn the power off to every floor one at a time. Doing this in descending order, five - four - three - two - one, he then walked out to his car leaving me with another salesperson standing in the dark. In a matter of minutes, before our eyes, the elevator turned itself on and started going up. I remember people stumbling over themselves to get out of the door—they were that scared! My father came back and locked the door, and we went home.

The next morning, salespeople went upstairs, and items were moved once again. None of this ever stopped, it only got worse, despite frequent mechanical checks. Even customers started to see and hear things.

A short while after this happened, the building was set for demolition by the City of Derby. We cleared everything out and moved to a new store. With the utilities turned off, they brought the massive cranes and bulldozers in to level the building. As the mighty building fell, part of the wall to the furniture building fell on the Commodore Hull building, collapsing the roof and people inside. Fortunately, there were minimal injuries but massive destruction. You can never tell if that was some sort of spirit acting up, or perhaps a curse. No one will ever

From the Collection of Michael James Mascolo

From the Collection of Michael James Mascolo

know. I did manage to take pictures that day of the building coming down and the destruction it caused. It took about a year to redo that part of the theater building. To this day it all seems very strange to me, but I guess things really do go bump in the night.

The Commodore Hull Theatre

My father purchased the Commodore Hull Theatre from Warner Brothers in 1958. Upon purchase of the theater, Warner Bros. did not allow any part of the theater left behind. They took out all the theater chairs, the curtains, projectors, and the lighting consoles, but they left the Wurlitzer pipe organ, which my father later sold. If you wander off Minerva Street, you might be able to take a glimpse inside the building. There are still paintings on the walls and murals depicting knights and dragons to liven up your experience in 1927.

The projection booth is still there, sticking out like a small fortress. The rest of the building was quite unique, however the lobby was turned into an appliance center while the theater itself turned into indoor parking. The stage was walled up, with floors put in for retail space.

One day in the early seventies, a group of us decided to take a tour of all the hidden spaces in the building, of which there are quite a few. We started in the basement and went down again into the boiler room where there is a service door to go even lower to get into the utility tunnels. They let stagehands move to the orchestra pit and the organ room. These rooms had been sealed off, with a roof placed over them for the parking area. These were tunnels with pipes and electrical conduit running through them and a dirt floor. So, the heat and electricity came out of the Minerva side to the Elizabeth side to heat the building.

While inspecting one of the tunnels, we came across a blue and white ruffled party dress, a pair of saddle shoes, a shovel, and a mound of dirt. Everyone thought it was a grave. This would be virtually in the middle of the floor of the theater building. Everyone came out of the tunnels and went to explain it to my uncle, who immediately called the police. I remember waiting in the boiler room while the police arrived, and my cousin escorted them to what everyone had found. I was quite a picture-taker back then and had been taking pictures everywhere in the building. The police, who were there quite a while, came out of the tunnels and told me and the rest of my family not to go in the tunnels anymore. They also took the film from my camera.

They were in and out of the tunnels for several days. Nobody ever revealed to us what they had found. I was told years later that they did find something, but I do not know if anything was removed. All these years later, I am sure nothing is probably left down there, but you never know! This is also another place which is scary and had numerous sightings by people parking their cars and going into the store. But it also could have been outside noises, as the building was acoustically built for the theater. To this day, if you clap your hands inside, you can hear the echo. The building was sold in 1980, and I know other property owners have gone down into these tunnels to remove parts of the organ's blower motors and whatnot. Even today, the building is still very mysterious.

The Sterling Opera House

Not being a firm believer in any of these hauntings or sightings, I would go up to the Opera House with others to explore. During this time, I didn't really see things, but maybe heard things. The Sterling

Opera House was built on 65-67 Elizabeth Street for Charles Sterling, who was already deceased. This Opera House was the show palace for the lower Naugatuck Valley. You can look up its history online or in the library archives.

There are even other articles on it in this book.

In brief, the building also housed the fire department, and up until the mid-sixties, the Derby Police Department. Most of my family were on the police force or were firefighters, and I would always hear stories from them about the Opera House. My aunt was a police officer there for over sixty years. I remember them always talking about things going on, of seeing and hearing things for many years, but you didn't really pay attention to it at the time. Even though they were police, who would you share the stories with who might've believed you? They'd tell you to go see a shrink!

Years ago, when the first group of paranormal ghost hunters went into the Opera House, I was talking to my aunt as we were watching it on TV. Here they were, searching for ghosts, and she turned to me and confessed that all of that was true, but no one would ever believe anyone on the force. The police department closed that facility sometime around the mid-sixties. It's a funny thing about all these reputedly haunted buildings, including the Adzima Funeral Home on Main Street, which was owned in the 1800s by the Vice President of Sterling Piano, that they all had Sterling pianos in them. The furniture store, the Commodore Hull Theatre (before the Wurlitzer was put in), the Opera House and the funeral home have all been said to be haunted.

The Ansonia Opera House

The Ansonia Opera House was owned by my Uncle Louis, another beautiful theater on the top floor of a much larger building. We used to go in there and clean it regularly.

Aside from doing maintenance, I had drum lessons there from 1967-1974 on the second floor. Whilst waiting for my lessons, I would go up to the theater and sit in the balconies' nice leather seats. While waiting for my turn to take lessons, I always had the feeling of someone watching me. I always figured it was my mind playing tricks on me; you're never really sure. In the late eighties, my uncle sold the building, but before we left, my uncle took the piano out of the Opera House. Yet

*Inside Ansonia Opera House, Early 2021.
Photo by Anthony Mullin, East Coast Paranormal Photography*

again, it was a Sterling piano. Maybe there is something in common with all these Sterling instruments, or maybe not.

Years ago, someone was nice enough to share with me correspondences between the Sterling family and their workers. I even have a letter opener from his desk. As an aside, relatives of the Sterling family were on the *Titanic*, coming back from England to New York.

It was cool having access to all these buildings when I was growing up and being able to explore. Might I have seen a few things, heard a few things? Is there some kind of tie-in with the Sterlings and these haunting? Through the years a lot of people can't be wrong.

The next time you hear that thump or someone talking, or you're seeing something from the corner of your eye, remember it could be a lost spirit trying to find his way home.

That's a *sterling* theory.

Michael James Mascolo was born and raised in Derby, where he served and is a past Captain of the Derby Fire Department, as were his brothers before him. His family settled in Derby in 1908, and went on to own and operate several businesses in the Valley, including such landmark buildings as the Commodore

Hull Theatre, James Furniture, and the Ansonia Opera House. He grew up spending much of his childhood in these buildings, as well as the Sterling Opera House, which was also the home of the Derby Police Department, where his relatives worked. He knew the ins and outs of all these businesses and theaters like the back of his hand, often exploring the tunnels beneath and the secret passageways. Some of these buildings are long gone, but their spirits remain. Mascolo still lives in the Valley, where he has been in the amusement/pinball business for four decades. His favorite pinball machines are "Haunted House" and "Class of 1812."

Michael James Mascolo meets four alien entities known as The Blue Man Group. From the Collection of Michael James Mascolo

DRAWING OUT THE ANSONIA OPERA HOUSE PHANTOMS

(If Derby's Sterling Opera House Deserved Two Chapters, Ansonia's Opera House Warrants One More as Well)

by Charles F. Rosenay!!!

In 2021, when I was invited to be part of an exploration inside Ansonia, Connecticut's Opera House, I jumped at the opportunity. It wasn't because I am the greatest of paranormal investigators, but because I am enamored with old theaters. When tourists go into a new city, they check out the museums or the restaurants. I look to find the baseball parks and the oldest theaters in town. If there's an original Fox or Warner or Palace Theater in a city, I try to look inside. If I can get into a shuttered or abandoned one, that's equally thrilling. When I have the opportunity to see one that's close to home, and I never thought I'd ever get inside, that's like striking gold. As for the Ansonia Opera House, I had driven by it countless times without even knowing it was there on Main Street in the city.

When my para-partner, Nick Grossmann, told me that we would be checking out the long-

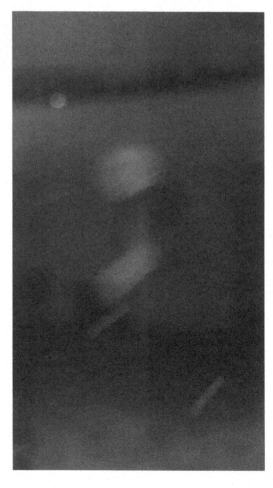

closed Ansonia Opera House with a few other investigators, including CT PASTS and our colleagues from East Coast Paranormal Photography, I was very excited.

They brought along all the proper equipment, meters, and tools of the trade, none of which I knew how to work. After the awe of the large, once-beautiful main room subsided, I proceeded to check out every room, every nook and cranny, and literally every inch of the building. It was majestic, but I felt nothing. No sounds, no ghosts, no spirits.

One of the more experienced investigators, who is far more sensitive, got rather sick for no apparent reason. When he made his way into a small area below the stage, he got nauseous and had to take a break.

I was taking photos on my camera, looking at them, and deleting them. That was going on for a while, when Nick told me to take some shots in the middle of the open room. It was in an area where patrons would have been sitting to watch shows, or, more specifically, in aisles where opera house guests might have walked to and from their seats. I don't know why Nick asked me to take photos then and there, but he said he sensed something.

I took a handful of photos, never expecting to have any results. What I captured was unbelievable. Along with a red orb, which I'm told is very rare, were two Nosferatu-looking spectral figures. You can see their pale white faces and bent arms as they are floating across the room! Herein is the photo I took, along with a closer look at the more pronounced phantom.

Later, when I returned home, I reviewed all the photos that I didn't erase off my phone. Sometimes you have to look twice before you delete pics. That's a lesson I learned.

There, in a wider shot of the interior of the opera hall, was a doorway. What I hadn't spotted was what had appeared right there in the doorway. You can judge for yourself.

DUDLEYTOWN EXPERIENCE

by Lisa Marie McKinney

It was the late seventies, and I was in my late teens. Neither myself, nor my friend, had ever heard of Dudleytown. My friend and I were taking a ride through Litchfield County to view the foliage. We had a cooler with some sandwiches and drinks for our lunch. I remember we were in the Mohawk Mountain area.

We ended up on some back roads where we saw a wooden sign nailed to a tree that simply said "PIG," with an arrow pointing to a turn in the road. We laughed at this, not knowing what it could mean, so we followed the arrow.

After following the arrow, we arrived at an empty field, with crumbling remnants of old stone walls and buildings. It was a beautiful, cloudless, sunny day. We decided to stop to eat our lunch there, but within several minutes, a black cloud came out of nowhere.

Suddenly, it began to rain, but it was not normal rain. The raindrops hit the windshield in big, thick syrupy drops, plopping on the windshield. Each raindrop was about three inches in diameter. I knew something wasn't right and got an instant chill up and down my spine.

Dudleytown group 2021. Photo by Charles F. Rosenay!!!

Another Dudleytown group 2021. Photo by Charles F. Rosenay!!!

The hairs on my arms were standing straight up. I also noticed there were no birds or insects at all.

With big, wide eyes I looked at my friend and she said, "Oh my God, it's blood." That was my thought too—even though the drops were clear like rain, they were definitely the consistency of blood! Immediately, my friend started the car and we left in fear. We didn't speak at all the whole way back to Waterbury and did not see another cloud in the sky anywhere.

About 10 years later, during the Halloween season, the *Waterbury Republican-American* newspaper ran a story about the legend of Dudleytown and the article included a map with the precise location. I immediately called the friend I was with and told her to check the newspaper. She called me back and said, "Oh my God, that's where we were that day!"

Natural born and hereditary, Lisa Marie McKinney is a professional psychic/medium, tarot master, clairvoyant (full range of psychic senses), knowledgeable in Astrology with 18 years of experience using her gifts for: In-person consultations / Phone consultations / Corporate and University events / Online chat readings / Skype webcam readings / Private parties / Astrology charts / Classes and workshops / Police investigations / Psychic Fairs / Radio and TV events / Medium circles & group events (similar format to TV psychic and medium John Edward). Lisa Marie has been laboratory tested and certified by a major university under the strictest scientific protocol. It is the same university that has tested many well known media psychics including, John Edward, Allison DuBois, and George Anderson. Ms. McKinney has also taught "Learning to Read the Tarot" and "Introduction to Astrology" at CT Adult Education.

DUDLEYTOWN REVISITED

by Charles F. Rosenay!!!

Growing up and hearing this town's name, I always thought of the cartoon character Dudley Do-Right. How scary could that be? When

The Shaman and The Showman: Nick Grossmann and Charles F. Rosenay!!! on their last Dudleytown adventure together

clairvoyant Nick Grossmann suggested we visit the notorious Dudleytown in Connecticut, I was intrigued, to say the least. After doing a little research, and hearing countless stories, as well as Nick's experiences, I felt we *had* to do something.

Dudleytown isn't even a proper town. It's an abandoned settlement in Cornwall, named after the Dudley family that settled there from England. Due to vandalism and trespassers, public owners have since closed the land and the site is not open to the public. Visitors to the site may even be subject to arrest for trespassing. You can read all about this ghost town in northwestern Connecticut on the internet.

Knowing a route that was legal and without trespassing, however, we brought an organized group hike to the site in 2021. Pictured is one of our groups. Each time, many of our guests had some very supernatural experiences.

On our first group visit, at one point, for no explicable reason, the hair on the head of one of the participants stood straight up for no reason as if he had an instant electrical charge. If truth be told, it was more like an entity was pulling his hair up in the air. He couldn't understand why we were all pointing to him until we took photos with our cell phones and showed him. To the left is the photo of the person who experienced this hair-raising experience (literally!).

Another guest saw what she described to the group as "a figure going by,

A Hair-Raising Scene. Photo by Traci Burton

across the forest, with a head of black." She further described it to us as a jogger or hiker with a black hood, black pants, black shirt, black everything; but quickly realized that there was nobody else in the woods except for us. She had seen a shadow creature in broad daylight.

Another participant from New Jersey named Traci, who had traveled to Connecticut to be part of this group exploration, was highly sensitive and felt a great pressure on her chest. Both she and the investigation leader, Nick Grossmann, felt and saw anomalies.

After our visit to Dudleytown, Traci wrote: "DudleyTown was incredible. I *never* had so much activity during the daytime. Crazy! Speaking of crazy, I saw the sun coming through the trees. I took a photo of it because it was pretty to me, but when I got home, I looked at it and I saw a tiffany blue mass at 5 o'clock to the sun. It's not the color of the sky and I'm not able to explain it. Did I capture something? Who knows?! But I can't explain it, nor did I see it when I took the picture."

More incredible might be the photo that captured the faces of elemental beasts in the center of the waterfalls looking upwards. See for yourself.

Look Closely at Elemental Beasts in the Waterfalls. Photo by Matt from Easton, CT

FAIRFIELD HILLS ASYLUM: SUBTERRANEAN JOURNEY TO THE UNDERWORLD

by Nick Grossmann

I'll never forget driving by this eerie building as a kid. Being a clairvoyant child was hard enough, but driving by a place of so many troubled souls was overwhelming. I remember seeing shadow entities standing on the campus of this eerie building and I watched them as we passed. I had no idea of the history of this location.

Years later, as a paranormal explorer, I heard of a place called Fairfield Hills Asylum. This sanitarium was notorious for testing medications on patients. They injected polio and hepatitis only to make lab rats of the mental patients. Hydrotherapy was a form of torture in some circles, and the medical staff believed it to be beneficial. What they would do is have a special bathtub specifically made for this style of treatment. They would then proceed to put the patient in and start with almost boiling hot water and let the patient sit in the tub. After

Interior Fairfield Hills Asylum. Photo by Nick Grossmann

about an hour of the hot water they would then replace it with freezing water. They believed the reaction would trick the brain into being well again. This was mild compared to the lobotomies and electric shock treatment used to destroy people's lives and turning them into borderline zombies. They would scrape the part of the brain by the forehead known as the pineal gland. Occasionally this treatment would actually help folks with extreme OCD, but, mostly, it just destroyed their lives, turning them into living vegetables!

Add the abuse that went on with the staff physically assaulting patients, patients committing suicide, and the countless numbers of "accidental" fatalities, and it's no surprise the number of tortured souls still haunting the grounds.

I have been a paranormal investigator for over two decades, but I recall when I first started to get curious about the facility. One Sunday I had time off and I decided to go to Fairfield Hills. I called my fellow explorers, but because everyone was busy that day, I decided to go by myself. After all, I've been seeing this stuff all my life; I'm pretty much used to it now.

I walked the trail into this abandoned abyss of shattered souls and went inside one of the buildings. There's nothing like the fresh smell of asbestos (?) to wake you up. As I proceeded to scope out the rest of the building, I kept seeing shadow figures walking everywhere. I went to the basement and found a tunnel. These tunnels used to cart dead bodies underground so the other patients wouldn't see the corpses and flip out. I walked through the tunnel and kept hearing footsteps follow me. As I reached about a third of the way, I turned around and saw a patient in a white hospital gown following me. I said, "Do you mind giving me some space?" The spirit stood there and just stared at me. I was very creeped out, to say the least. After all, doing paranormal research like this by yourself is a much different ball game than doing it in a group with peers. I turned and said I had enough of this and walked out of the tunnel, being followed all the way back down.

As I got to the basement, I kept hearing conversations, but no one was there. I returned to the upstairs level, and all the sudden all the doors and windows were slamming violently. I got so freaked out I ran up the stairs and dove out through an open window. My heart was racing.

Corridor Inside Fairfield Woods Asylum. Photo by Nick Grossmann

An interesting fact about Fairfield Hills is the occult worship that has gone on there for years. In abandoned asylums, you see occult worship everywhere, but Fairfield Hills was infested with it. These practitioners of dark magick go to these places, and because there are so many troubled souls, they see it as an opportunity to perform necromancy rituals and make spirits do things for them.

Once I made my way into another building on the campus at night. I walked up stairs only to meet two beheaded pigeons. I remember thinking how weird it was that they were just lying there. As I walked the hallway, I found literally a maze of isolation rooms. I stumbled across a room with a hydrotherapy bathtub in it. There was an upside-down pentacle spray-painted on the walk with blood smeared all over it. I can't deny the fact of how fascinating it was, even though it creeped me the hell out. I wasn't alone that time, and as we proceeded further into the realm, there was a building infested with bats. Bravely enough, we went through the bat-infested building. The bats were flying into our faces because they had no ecosystem locations. Normally, they would never land on us.

The destination where we were headed turned out to be the prayer room of the asylum. Most big asylums had churches in them but this one was different as an occult group had clearly taken it over and transformed it into their own house of worship. There was one way in and one way out. This area had a giant pentacle on the ground with a bunch of used candles. There was graffiti everywhere, and one of my colleagues started to read the messages on the walls. I told him to stop reading it. As an explorer, I learned to be careful reading graffiti because they can actually be spells that the occult groups spray up on the walls so you will get cursed if they're read aloud.

Fairfield Hills Asylum is the most terrifying yet fascinating place I have been to both for historic reasons and for its paranormal content.

Nick Grossmann is the real deal. He has been clairvoyant his entire life and is dedicated to the paranormal field. One half of "The Shaman and The Showman" (along with the author of this book), the "shaman" has traveled extensively, has performed exorcisms and cleansings, and has collected some of the rarest haunted artifacts and antiquities from North America and overseas. His valuable collection includes a cursed, personal item from the infamous Aleister Crowley, which was on display at ParaConn, the first ever Paranormal Convention in Connecticut, of which Nick was executive producer and the co-host. Nick's organization, Ghost Storm, continues his goal to *"prove the paranormal."* He produces videos with supernatural evidence and leads ghost hunts and investigations year-round. He is also the host of theater presentations where the audience participates in an evening of the supernatural, including scrying sessions and other interactive attractions. www.TheShamanandTheShowman.com.

GREEN LADY CEMETARY

by Tommy Dreivers

My name is Tommy Dreivers and I'm a paranormal investigator from Massachusetts. In May of 2021, my group and another group of investigators were at Green Lady Cemetery in Burlington, Connecticut. We were not entirely sure what was going to happen, or what we were going to run into, but what happened certainly caught us all by surprise.

About an hour into the investigation, it began to get dark out and we started setting up our equipment. We had EVPs, spirit boxes, and motion light balls around the cemetery. Shortly after dark, we started getting some activity. I felt a presence behind, and above me in the tree that I was standing next to. After that, I felt a constant feeling of being watched.

All the other investigators at the cemetery started getting odd feel-

Cemetery Photo courtesy Tommy Dreivers

ings of being watched as well, and they could see something was especially bothering me. They started checking on me periodically, as they saw me start wandering around.

Later in the night, I started feeling a much darker presence beyond the stone wall surrounding us. Whatever was in the woods, I felt as if it wanted to hurt me or the others, but it seemed to be focused more on me. This dark spirit started staring at me with deep eye contact. Everyone saw me just standing there looking into the woods, and then I actually fainted from the energy it put out.

I got up after a few minutes, not really knowing what just happened, but then it all came back to me. We ended up gathering our gear and packing up for the night.

Everyone made sure I was okay before I drove home and I contacted my group once I made it home safe.

HAUNTED AT HOME

by Paul Longo, Jr.

In the mid-nineties, our parents moved us to a new house in Stratford, Connecticut. We had regular unexplained experiences during my entire time living there, and my parents, who still reside there, have occasional visits from the other side.

My interest has always been with storytelling. My intention is never to convince anyone of anything one way or another—but to simply tell the story as I know it, and let the audience come to its own conclusion. The reason why my childhood home is my go-to for tales of hauntings is because so many others have also had experiences there. It is easy to debunk the experiences of one lone paranormal enthusiast but hearing the accounts of others from the same location adds much weight to a story.

My older sister had her bedroom in a backroom that we called "the office." On multiple occasions, she would wake up to a room full of fog. She recounts many occasions of waking up to what looked like the room filled with a white smoke, with no logical explanation as to why. On other occasions she would wake up to find the window and door leading to the outside wide open (as this room was once an office, it had a doorway leading outside).

She also tells of a recurring dream about a presence that felt pure evil. The creature wouldn't let her leave the room—she would make it as far as the door and it would hold her back and refuse to let her leave.

My younger sister is plagued by an experience she didn't even know she had. To get to the bathroom, you had to pass her bedroom through the hallway. One night, a friend was sleeping over and got up to use the bathroom. Upon passing her room, he saw a shadow figure standing over her while she slept. The next morning, he told her about it, and it scared her for life. This remains one of the scariest memories she has.

My mother and father have conceded to the idea that the house is haunted. One day, my mother was home by herself. There was a loud banging noise from downstairs, so she went to investigate. She walked into the kitchen to see the cordless house phone spinning on the kitchen counter. There would have been no time for someone to randomly spin the phone and run out of the house in the time it took her to come down the stairs (and honestly—if someone broke into the house just to do that it is equally as frightening).

The same day as I am writing this, I got a video from my mother. She was able to record a flashlight on the bed-stand going on and off on its own in the middle of the night. Even after inspecting the flashlight and replacing the batteries, it continues to happen (we are trying to convince her to talk to the possible spirit and see if it will communicate directly through the turning of the light on).

Even my father—who is probably the most skeptical of the group of us—can confess to an unexplained experience he had within the house. One day he went into the garage and got in his car on his way to work. As he sat in the car in the garage, in the rearview mirror, he saw someone walk behind the car. Immediately concerned and confused as to why someone was in the garage, he checked the side view mirrors and then got out to look. No one was there.

Haunted Home. Photo by Paul Longo Jr.

I could probably find 15 people to recount having this next experience. While standing in certain areas of the kitchen, you could see the bay window in the living room. On a regular occasion, a man would be seen standing at the window. It looked as if he was standing inside and watching out the window—as if waiting for someone. We jokingly began calling him Stanley (the name of the previous homeowner who was elderly and ill at his time of moving out). If you were hanging out at the house and decided to leave for the night, it was a good probability you would see Stanley standing by the window when you left the kitchen and turned the corner.

Concluding with my personal experiences... For as early as I can remember, I always had unsettling dreams in this house. A recurring dream was about a creature who lived in the toy box of my closet. In my dream, I would be alone in the house, and it was completely dark. No lights were on at all, except for the one light in my closet. I would walk towards it with extreme apprehension and fear, and as soon as I entered the closet, the toy box would pop open, and a terrible creature would jump out at me.

In some dreams, he chased me into the dark. In others, everything would go black as soon as he caught me in the closet.

We had an unfinished basement which, for years, was the local hangout for our friends. We had everything we needed to stay down there for the entire weekend. Every Friday and Saturday night, there were no vacant couches. We stayed up all night and everyone found a place to sleep, and we would repeat this process for weeks and weeks. The basement was divided into half – one side for our hangout and the other for storage. We hung sheets from the rafter to create a physical divide in the room.

One night I woke up abruptly and was immediately fixated on the sheet leading into the storage area. After a short period of time, I saw someone pass through the sheet. The fabric moved as if someone walked through, but the entity was invisible. I was struck with fear and rolled over to try to fall back asleep (If you go to sleep it goes away. Right?). I took a quick glance and saw one of my friends laying wide awake with a petrified look on his face and eyes wide open. He mouthed to me "did you see that?" I nodded my head and somehow went back to sleep. We still talk about this night, close to 15 years later.

My name is Paul Longo, and I am a Connecticut resident. From my early childhood, listening to tales of the paranormal and unknown has been a great interest of mine. Everywhere I go, I find myself talking to someone and hearing their unexplainable ghost stories. Recently, I began a paranormal magazine to spotlight ghost stories and urban legends. Each issue contains stories from readers, some local, some from the other side of the world. You can learn more about reading (and contributing to this zine) at <u>www.ghostwatch.us.</u>

HAUNTED BY HISTORY: THE CURTIS HOUSE

by Leanna Renee Hieber

As an actress, playwright, lecturer, ghost tour guide, and author of over fifteen paranormal, ghost-filled novels, my friends know by now that a good ghost story is the quickest way to my heart. Considering that most of my novels are set in the 19th century, if you can't tell me a ghost story, then show me a historic building. Extra points if it's a *haunted* historic building.

One of my dearest friends, author A. L. Davroe, lives in Connecticut and for the past many years, I've had the pleasure of visiting often. I've also been a part of Oddball Newt's Steampunk events for many seasons, allowing me the opportunity to visit many wonderful historic spaces through the years.

An experience at Woodbury, Connecticut's The Curtis House Restaurant and Inn (not to be confused with the Curtiss House in Trumbull) stands out as both pleasant and compelling. A.L. Davroe specifically took me to the Inn because not only does it have a reputation for being haunted, it's also a charming restaurant that has great comfort food.

Outside Sally's Room: Haunted Room #16 at the Curtis House.
Photo by Leanna Renee Hieber

Win-win.

After a delicious meal in the dining room, a staff member kindly guided us around the Inn part of the historic complex and showed us a few of the most notably haunted spaces, all maintained in a historic setting with antique furniture and a light, airy atmosphere.

Curtis House Stairs and Hall. Photo by Leanna Renee Hieber

Room #16 stood out to me; said to be haunted by the ghost of a young girl, nicknamed Sally, whose history isn't entirely clear. Numerous reports through the years detail a playful and sometimes rambunctious young spirit who has a penchant for bedclothes. Whether pulling on them or tucking guests in, she's particularly attentive to the covers. Some guests she may favor, others she might pester a bit. Harmless, but rather surprising if your bedsheets shift on their own.

I've always been aware of areas and structures that have a certain spectral resonance to them. I could definitely tell that The Curtis House is a haunted location. There's an odd sort of weight, something about the air, an ineffable quality about the sound and light.

Haunted buildings can take on a metaphysical quality that becomes very hard to describe, but something that sensitives can absolutely feel. A sixth sense does defy the other five and will vary from person to person. Hauntings, like art, are subjective.

The general feeling of The Curtis House isn't an unsettled one. Even if the spirits have unfinished business, it doesn't keep the building from feeling welcoming. No matter how many ghosts might wander about the place, it seems that the spirits mostly get along with visitors and locals, especially those who are respectful of the premises and its history.

The Curtis House is a rare example of an 18th century Inn, founded as such, that has remained in continuous usage and in family hands for the duration of its history. All the more appealing for a spirit who might wish for things to remain exactly as they have been. The Inn is noted in many haunted house directories. Their tag-line is apt: "Every Modern Comfort, Every Ancient Charm." Ghosts don't much like change, and The Curtis House has maintained a warm balance of history in our modern world. It's worth a visit to step one foot in the past while living in the present; my favorite kind of encounter.

Leanna Renee Hieber is an actress, playwright, ghost tour guide, and the award-winning, bestselling author of over fifteen gothic, gaslamp fantasy, and supernatural suspense novels for adults and teens for Tor, Sourcebooks and Kensington Books, as well as the "Dark Nest" space opera novellas for Scrib'd. Her debut non-fiction, "A Haunted History of Invisible Women: True Stories of America's Ghosts," co-authored with Andrea Janes, examines women's narratives in haunted houses and ghost stories around the country.

Her "Strangely Beautiful" saga, beginning with "The Strangely Beautiful Tale of Miss Percy Parker," hit Barnes & Noble and Borders Bestseller lists and garnered numerous regional genre awards. Tor Books notes "Strangely Beautiful" as a "foundational text of Gaslamp Fantasy" and new, revised editions are now available via Tor. "Darker Still" hit American Bookseller's Association's 'Indie Next List" and was a Scholastic Book Club 'Highly Recommended' title and a Daphne du Maurier award finalist. She lectures on Gothic fiction and ghostly themes for prominent institutions such as New York University and at conventions, libraries, and conferences around the country.

A proud member of Actors Equity and SAG-AFTRA, Mystery Writers of America, SFWA, Historical Novel Society, International Thriller Writers, and The Dramatists Guild, Leanna lives in New York where she is a licensed NYC tour guide working with Boroughs of the Dead and has been featured in film and television on shows like "Boardwalk Empire" and "Mysteries at the Museum." She tours a one-woman show as 19th century designer Clara Driscoll and is represented by Paul Stevens of the Donald Maass agency. She tweets often @leannarenee. Website: http://leannareneehieber.com

HOOKMAN'S CEMETERY
THINGS FOLLOW. THINGS ATTACH.

by Jeffrey Gerry

Being autistic, the roads have always been enormously bumpy. I've needed to shift responsibilities constantly, as it's easy to get overloaded, and melt down with things as simple as calling a client. In turn, it made it that much easier to organize a dedicated team with dedicated roles to handle all the aspects of working a case.

There have been many cases over the years ranging from mild to extreme. From investigating alongside the TAPS team (from *Ghost Hunters*), to presenting at the anniversary event alongside Lorraine Warren at the Mark Twain House, it's been a wild ride so far. Some investigations definitely stand out more than others, and this is one of those prime examples.

Long before founding the team, there were events in place that cemented the absolute need to know more about the other side. I was

Hookman's Cemetery. Photo by Jeffrey Gerry

always targeted as a child. I heard things in my grandmother's old house bouncing down the attic stairs. I had a battery-less remote-control car drive itself off the table when I was five years old, and the closet door handle would shake violently in that very same house. Things like this target you; follow you, when you're sensitive to them—and once they know you can hear or see them, they will never stop.

This brings me to one terrible night. I was significantly younger at the time and far less experienced. I thought it would be a phenomenal idea to walk to a cemetery to record some audio and take some photos. The location was Hookman's Cemetery in Seymour, Connecticut.

The walk to Hookman's Cemetery in Seymour took maybe two hours on a dark, clear night. Upon finally getting there, my cousin and I could not even enter the cemetery. It was different that night than ever before. There were noises throughout all the surrounding woods. Rustling, crashing, whispering. We just couldn't walk in. We stood at the gates taking it in, and inevitably thought it best to turn around and walk the long distance back home.

A few minutes after heading in the opposite direction down the dark stretch of road, something felt . . . off. We both stopped walking to evaluate. That's when it all became clear. Piercing the absolute silence that night, a third set of footsteps stopped walking a couple of seconds behind ours. Being new to the field and inexperienced, no precautions were taken beyond simply leaving the area. It was a mistake.

Upon arriving home, I settled in for bed, and my cousin went home to his house. I woke up to a whisper in my ear, that had to be no less than a couple feet away. "I won't let you rest." Barely awake, I opened my eyes to see an old traffic cone I had sitting in the room had been tipped over and was inches from my eye. There was a pounding at my back door less than five minutes later. My cousin was woken out of his sleep as well, and upon waking up and heading upstairs, he turned around to see a young girl following him up from the basement.

There was no further sleep that night.

Things follow, things attach.
Whatever it was on that particular night has stuck with us since.
Precautions to protect yourself need to be put in place. If someone warns you that a place may be dangerous, please believe that dangers

are not always of the visible nature and proceed with knowledge and caution.

In an update to this, my cousin still sees her appear to him, although less frequently, and she has aged from that little girl to a young woman. In my case, I consulted a psychic advisor in Gettysburg, who informed me that this passenger was not human and goes by the name "Castor," and that its preferred method of communication was squealing like a pig, and occasionally appearing as a wispy black cat.

This brings everything back to the primary point here. We strive to protect people from danger and help people realize that things you wouldn't think to be dangerous—entering a cemetery and just recording for a few minutes—could have consequences that follow for years. We formed to assist those in need of help without ridicule or bias, and just help them rest at night, knowing that they are not alone in their struggles.

Jeffrey Gerry has led an interesting life. As he tells it, "I am diagnosed autistic and constantly struggle to find my way. I did find my calling in 2007, the year I founded my paranormal team CTPASTS (the Connecticut Paranormal and Supernatural Tracking Society). Our goal has always been to assist people in need and help rid them of unwanted spirits in their homes or businesses"

MEETING ED AND LORRAINE WARREN

by Steve Biff Saunders

On a Sunday afternoon in the early nineties the phone rang at my restaurant Biff's Place, in Prospect, Connecticut. A lady on the other end of the phone asked if the owner was there, and I replied, "Speaking." She asked me if there was any activity going on in my restaurant. I chuckled when I replied that I had three banquet halls and I had a lot of activity going on there.

She replied with, "No sir, the supernatural kind."

I responded back with a simple, "Yes there is."

She went on to inform me that her name was Lorraine Warren and that her husband's name was Ed and that they were paranormal investigators. She asked me if it would be okay to come to my restaurant with her team. I told her that of course they could come on down. At that point in my life I had not yet told anybody about any of my own gifts.

We set up a time during the week approximately when there would not be much business going on at the location. They arrived and they set up in the middle banquet hall upstairs.

Lorraine broke out a notepad, opened it up, and started to call out, "Cameraman number one?"

The response was, "Camera batteries dead. EVP meters dead."

She called out, "Camera number two" and the reply came, "Camera number two battery is dead."

This went on and I asked her why she did not charge her batteries before getting to my location, and in a stern and direct voice, she commented, "We fully charged our batteries before we left our location. Are you aware that spirits drain batteries?"

At that point I was a newbie and learning everything hands-on.

She then asked me to take her to the hot spot. I asked her what a hotspot was? Her reply was a bit sarcastic, "Where you feel things." Off we went to one of the locations and she asked if there was another place and I brought her there as well. Her husband asked her if she was okay, and she replied that she was just going to take care of the basics and get out. It should be noted that it was as if she had Tourette's

Syndrome, with her reactions while looking around at the activity she was able to see.

She asked me a couple questions and then she pushed out in her voice firmly, "Oh my god—you are a sensitive." I told her I knew I was sensitive.

Her response was, "No, not sensitive—a sensitive!" She asked me if I even knew what that meant. I did not. I didn't know that my gifts had a name. Lorraine said, "It's okay, I have the gift, my husband has the gift, half of my team has the gift." She then called out to the cameraman to bring over the tripod, the camcorder, and an electrical cord to plug it in because the batteries were dead.

She conducted a fifteen-minute interview with me which was in their museum under the title "Prospect Restaurant." I never saw a copy of that evening and the events they documented.

Lorraine left the building, and it was time for Ed and the crew to go into the hotspot that made me feel uncomfortable. I had a Pitbull named Boo Boo with a 24-inch neck, and he would not want to go into that room. We went into what were the old showers for the pool area on the back side of the restaurant, currently used for one of the furnaces to keep the bar warm. This room was blacker than black, and you could not even see your hand in front of your face. As we were in there a little dark creature started moving around the floor space up against the wall. Ed asked me to speak to it.

I said, "No, it's not my friend. I have nothing to say to it. I just bought this place."

Moments later, a tall dark spirit (at the time I thought it was a person) moved across in front of me. Thinking it could have been one of the members of the team, I reached out, and my arm went through it cold as ice. I hooted like a little girl.

Ed commented that if I was scared, I could leave. I said, "No, please tell me you guys are seeing what I'm seeing." A few moments later Ed asked me if he could put out holy water.

As he was spraying out the holy water the room started to lighten up, and I was starting to be able to see all the entities that were just moments ago pitch. I asked Ed and the others if they saw what I was seeing with this room getting lighter? You could feel a tension in the air ease up and the fear dissipate. Mission accomplished, darkness gone.

It was a pleasure to meet Ed and Lorraine Warren and their team. I did not know who they were at the time. I don't know if you'll believe this or not, but Lorraine Warren follows me in the paranormal work that I do and is one of my biggest fans. It's quite impressive that the woman who met me many years ago now hangs with me, even after she has passed. I'm sure that she most likely hangs with some of you guys as well.

Steve Biff Saunders lives in Torrington, Connecticut, where he is an empath, intuitive, healer, terminator of negative energies and more. While weathering the storm of these gifts, he came to the realization that many people are struggling with the unknown, and he offers healing and relief for those suffering.

THEY WHO WALKED AMONG US: MIDDLETOWN CONNECTICUT VALLEY HOSPITAL

by Anthony Mullin

Could you imagine walking the halls of an abandoned hospital while it was still in operation?

A team of explorers visited this location in the hopes of getting some great photos of the area but got a little more than they expected.

While exploring, two photographers who had separated from the

Photo by East Coast Paranormal Photography

main group experienced some strange occurrences. They were hearing voices and loud footsteps above them. When they went to see if anyone was there and called out, they didn't get any response, nor did they find anyone walking around. Later they discovered that they were the only people in the building—the rest of the group were in separate buildings or in tunnels beneath the hospital.

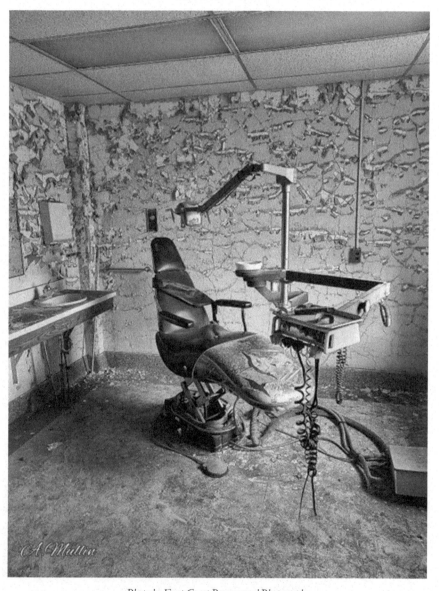

Photo by East Coast Paranormal Photography

When you know the history of a location like this and actually get a chance to walk the same hallways as the doctors and patients, and when you're passing old records, hospital beds, and wheelchairs that are over one hundred years old, you can almost feel the heaviness and sadness left behind by the spirits that still roam those halls.

Since 2019, East Coast Paranormal Photography explores and captures what may have been forgotten but not gone, in an effort to bring awareness and history to the forefront.

Joey Febus, Katie Hoye, Anthony Mullin of East Coast Paranormal Photography

MY WARRENS STORY

by Charles F. Rosenay!!!

I loved and respected Ed and Lorraine Warren before the world knew them. If you're from Connecticut, you probably did too. The Warrens would appear regularly at schools and theaters, including my alma mater, Southern Connecticut State University. Their presentation was always fun, scary, and fascinating. People in the area were fortunate to be able to see them often, especially around Halloween time, when they were doing their shows everywhere.

When my tour operation business was starting to expand, and the Dracula Tours to Transylvania I was promoting and hosting were selling out annually, many of the travelers were clamoring for more theme tours. My best friend and business partner at the time, Danny Levine, encouraged me to expand the "tours of terror" beyond Romania. It only made sense to do other similarly themed trips, but to different destinations. We decided the first one should be a GHOSTour to England, and we both started brainstorming on who could be potential "haunted hosts" to join us on these pilgrimages.

If you're connecting the dots, you can guess who we thought would make for the perfect hosts of these haunted vacations. We contacted Ed and Lorraine and arranged a meeting to explain our new vacation venture. The Warrens invited us to come over to their home and discuss everything. I was out of the country, so Danny visited them at their home in Monroe, Connecticut.

Ed Warren and my friend hit it off immediately. They both loved to talk, and while Danny told Ed of all the tours and productions we put on, Ed told Danny about his and Lorraine's adventures. After some time just schmoozing, Ed asked Danny if he wanted to see the haunted artifacts they'd collected over the years. Here's where it gets interesting.

They walked together down into the basement where The Warrens stored "souvenirs" of their investigations, exorcisms, and cleansings. It was like a macabre mini-museum. Danny remarked that Ed was very proud of the artifacts and pointed out the ones that were the most "active," as well as the ones that were the most dangerous.

I don't recall if Lorraine was at home when Danny arrived, but she probably had left as Danny was touring the cellar, because the phone rang, and Ed said he had to grab it. The phone was upstairs in the home. Ed and Danny and the haunted artifacts were downstairs. Ed told Danny to just stay still, that he wouldn't be long. But he added, "And don't go near that one no matter what—it's locked up." He pointed to a large glass case which contained, or, rather, imprisoned, an otherwise normal-looking doll.

The doll under lock and key happened to be the infamous Annabelle doll.

"The Shaman and The Showman," Nick Grossmann and Charles F. Rosenay!!! at the Warrens' gravesite in Stepney, Connecticut, 2021.

Danny didn't give it much thought as Ed went up the stairs to get the phone call. Danny looked around for a few seconds before he heard a click sound. He turned in the direction of Annabelle just as the front of the locked glass door opened. Yes, it was locked and it opened up by itself.

I need to tell you two things. One was that Danny wasn't scared by many things. Two was that Danny didn't move fast. When the Annabelle doll's glass casing opened, Danny literally flew up the stairs to join Ed, who was chatting away on the phone. Danny told me he never moved so fast in his life.

When his heart stopped palpitating, he and Ed discussed the possibilities of them joining us as tour hosts. Ed felt that he and Lorraine were getting too old to travel, but he recommended John Zaffis as someone who would be great in their place. We didn't wind up working with Zaffis, who went on to a very successful paranormal career in his own right, but we both agreed that Lorraine was special in so many ways, and it would have been amazing to have had them along for at least one of our GHOSTour adventures.

Although I saw them live at events many times, and almost toured with them, I never visited Lorraine or Ed Warren in their home. I never descended into their basement, and I never was privy to Ed leaving me alone with the Annabelle doll. That's okay. Danny's visit was good enough for the both of us. I do, however, visit the Warrens' gravesite to pay my respects.

This chapter was for you, Danny.

NEW CANAAN'S POSSESSED LADY

by Hector Roque

I am a paranormal videographer and I accompany teams on their investigations to try and capture the encounters and phenomenon.

I went on one of my first cases awhile back. Before that, I watched a lot of paranormal TV shows in the past and while they were compelling and entertaining, I always felt they were a bit exaggerated. When Nick Grossmann of the Ghost Storm texted me and said that we are dealing with a possession scenario I was immediately skeptical.

The time came to investigate and see what was truly going on. Joining Nick and me on this investigation was Anthony DiPietro, with Jeff Gerry and Diane Berti from CT PASTS. Some of the team had met the women in question before, but not me.

When I met her, my first impressions were that she seemed very nice, but she seemed drained, overwhelmed, and tired. She told us that she has been kept up several nights due to an overwhelming energy. She also claimed to be getting possessed by an older lady spirit.

I could definitely tell she was having some problems. While Nick and Anthony were interviewing her, Jeff, Diane, and I went upstairs to investigate. We found lots of mysteries and interesting, possible conclusions about the case.

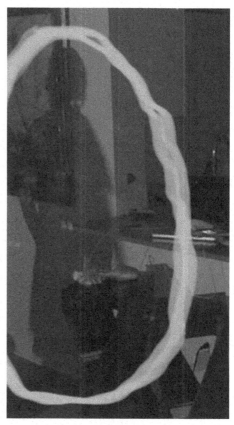

Shadow of the Spirit that possessed the Lady.
Photo by Hector Roque

What really stood out was the evidence I had captured. For starters I had taken a photo in a mirror and in it was the shadow of the spirit that she had said had possessed her. Note the strange white eyes that peer down.

While recording I also captured what had seemed to be an apparition of a dove flying in front of my camera. Nick had also recorded a video of a black mask in the reflection in the mirror.

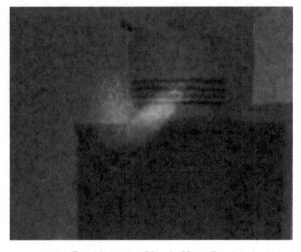

Dove Apparition. Photo by Hector Roque

In the investigation we tried to communicate with the spirits by doing a séance. While everyone was participating, I tried to be as silent as possible as I walked around and filmed them all. While this was happening, I could hear voices downstairs, as if people were communicating with each other.

The case is ongoing.

Since becoming part of this team, I pay more attention to the normal and abnormal things most people don't. I find myself being more drawn to and fascinated by the unknown, and the supernatural activity that surrounds me.

NEW-GATE PRISON

by Larry and Debbie Elward

Larry and I went to Old New-Gate Prison in East Granby, Connecticut in June of 2021. The prison was founded in 1773 as a prison even though the area had underground copper mines. The prisoners consisted mostly of burglaries, forgery, and counterfeiting. Prisoners were used as forced laborers to mine the mines. It was used until 1827 when prisoners were transferred to the new Wethersfield state prison. Effort was made to continue mining until about 1850 when it was abandoned and sold as a tourist attraction.

It is now a museum and a very haunted locale.

On our visit there, I was able to discern a very heavy atmosphere in the jail area. We decided to try EVPs to see if we could get any messages. We actually

Old New-Gate Prison Outdoor Sign
Photo by Larry and Debbie Elward

Old New-Gate Prison Interior.
Photo by Larry and Debbie Elward.

got one EVP that said "purgatory" when we asked where the spirit was. We also got some SLS pictures inside as well. At one point during the day the court felt like there was a lot of energy there even though Larry and I were the only ones there.

It is a very active place, and one that Connecticut paranormal investigators should visit, but it's not our best experience. That would be…

NIGHT AT THE CONJURING HOUSE THE NEXT STATE OVER

by Larry and Debbie Elward

Larry and I had been invited to participate in a seance at the Farm on Round Top Road or, as it's better known, the Conjuring House (of the Warner Brothers *Conjuring* film franchise). The seance was to be conducted the night before Halloween and was billed as a follow up seance to the one that Ed and Lorraine Warren did in the 1970s.

Of course, we were excited at the possibilities. Imagine spending the night at one of America's most haunted houses.

This house is not the house that is shown in the movie. Rather, it's a 14-room Cape Cod home that was built in the early 1800s. The home is furnished as if you have stepped back into the 1800s which adds to the haunted feel of the home.

The Conjuring House. Photo by Larry and Debbie Elward

Inside The Conjuring House. Photo by Larry and Debbie Elward

The night started off with a tour of the home that included the cellar. This is a dark area that has an energy that seems to hold many secrets especially around the old well where there had been many reports of entities crawling out of it. We did not witness that, but we did have strange feelings of the room swaying as if we were on a ship.

Next was time for the seance which was conducted in the same area as the Warrens had done many years previous. All participants sat around a table as the spirits were invited to attend. Soon there were reports of shadow people in the adjacent rooms as well as a sighting of ghost children peeking in the windows.

Audible footfalls and knocking were heard by everyone assembled around the table. The smoke from the candles and incense began to swirl around everyone's heads as the sound of wood splintering could be heard, everyone was shocked to see the table begin to separate with each sound. Soon things began to settle down and all activity died down for the time being. The participants left and we were one of the lucky ones to get to spend the night.

Our room was on the second floor, and you could feel the house settle down somewhat, but not fully rest. It was as if it were waiting, maybe for all to let their guard down. As soon as we fell asleep, I woke up sometime in the middle of the night. The room was very cold, and I was shivering from it. Instinctively I knew someone, or something was in our room, but I chose not to look.

I could hear Larry sleeping soundly and then I heard a grandfather clock somewhere in the house start to chime. It went halfway down the scale and stopped and bonged one time and I instantly fell back to sleep. Not to be disturbed again until morning.

In the morning the host asked how we slept, and I told him the story of waking up and the clock. Our host took us into the area where the seance had taken place and there was the grandfather clock standing in the corner. Except that it was only the cabinet with no inner workings. so it could not have chimed in the middle of the night.

This house still holds on to its secrets; maybe it is waiting for just the right person to unlock them.

Larry and Debbie Elward have been in the paranormal field for many years, working respectively as priest and psychic. Both started with Ed and Lorraine Warren and have continued more recently with "The Haunted Collector" himself—John Zaffis—but frequently assist other groups as well. Larry and Debbie have both been on several TV shows, such as: "A Haunting," "The Haunted," "Unsolved Mysteries," the UK's "Jane Goldman Presents" and "Connecticut's "Greg Dwyer's After Dark." Together with John Zaffis, they've released their first book, "What Lurks Within" which won "Paranormal Rewind's Best Paranormal Book of 2020." Their second book is nearing completion, and may even be out by the time the book you're holding is published.

ON NOVA SCOTIA HILL

by Angela Marie

I've been to Dudleytown, Union Cemetery, and Fairfield Hills. I walked through Little People Village many times as a child and explored the haunted barn in Woodbury, Connecticut. I've been lucky enough to explore the Warner Theater, and I've also sat in the jail cells at the Sterling Opera House in Derby. Being a paranormal investigator, I was lucky enough to visit and have experiences in all these locations. Not one of them compares to living in my childhood home on Nova Scotia Hill Rd in Watertown, Connecticut.

I was 19 years old and still living at home with my parents. I had just returned from college for my Thanksgiving break. As usual, I was nervous to come home. Growing up in my childhood home was extremely stressful because of the paranormal activity that was happening. It always seemed to center around my mother and me. There were disembodied voices, shadow figures that would walk through my bedroom, tapping noises, growls, scratches, and my sister's bed shook up off the floor once.

On this particular night, I went to bed in a pair of red and white-checkered boxers and a white short-sleeved T-shirt that said the word "Cheer" across it. Before I talk about what happened next, I have to say that at this point in my life, I was very aware that my mother and I had two completely different beliefs when it came to religion. My mother is a Born-Again Christian while I had very much accepted my Strega roots.

I went to bed at 10 PM. I wasn't feeling so good that day. I had a head cold and I really couldn't breathe out of my nose. I was all congested and achy and had a low-grade fever. I curled up into my twin bed which was pushed up against the wall in the corner. It was in the corner because I knew that if I put pillows on the other side of me, then maybe I wouldn't feel like someone was trying to touch me in the middle of the night (which was normal because of the paranormal activity in that home). I fell asleep pretty fast. The exhaustion from being sick had totally knocked me out. I suddenly opened my eyes, and

I was standing in the woods. At first, I was a little bit confused. I didn't know where I was. My parents had about an acre of land before you hit the tree line where my father owned 3-4 more acres.

When I turned around, I saw that the lights from the house looked very small. I looked down and I could see that my feet were bare. I could see my white T-shirt that said "Cheer" on it. I could also feel the leaves and sticks under my feet. But I noticed something strange—I wasn't breathing. I looked around again, and I realized that at that moment I wasn't in my body.

I had read about astral projection as a child, but this was different. There was no silver cord. So I started to get scared because I thought to myself, "am I dead?" That's when an overwhelming fear came over me. I felt the urgency to run. To run away from my parents' house as fast as I possibly could. So that's what I did. I ran. I could feel the leaves and the sticks and the rocks under my feet. I could also feel a cold breeze that was coming at me. And then I heard something running behind me.

At first, I didn't know what it was, so I kept running. I was too afraid to look back. It was the strangest feeling in the world. Normally, when you're running, you're taking deep breaths and exerting yourself to keep going, but that wasn't what was happening here. I didn't know where I was pulling the energy from. It just felt as if I was being propelled by something different. That "something" felt more natural than oxygen. I ran and it got darker and darker.

When I finally turned around, I could see that what was chasing me was much larger than me. It looked to be about eight to nine feet tall. It appeared to be a black smoke that had formed into a body that was covered in a cloak. I kept running and running, wondering why I could not just hear it, but also feel it running after me. But there was no noise coming from anything except the sounds of its "feet." Then I heard another set of feet. And my mother's voice.

My mother started screaming, "*Run, Angela, run!* Don't look back, Angela. Keep running! It almost has you!" I looked back and there was my mother running after this being that was running after me. I saw my mom's white nightgown and bare feet, and then I turned forward and kept running.

Then, my mother was screaming, 'Wake up Angela! Wake up!" At that moment, I sat up in my bed. Pillows knocked to the floor as my mother burst through my bedroom door and flipped on the light. She was out of breath. She looked at me and said, "Angela, I just had the most terrible dream that we were in the woods behind the house and that you were being chased by a demon in a black cloak." I looked at her and said, "I know, Mom. I saw you."

At the time, I had no explanation for what had happened that night. To this day, my mother will always ask, "Where were we?" And I always answer her and say, "I don't know, Mom." But what I do know is that those hooded figures sometimes still show up in our dreams. Even though my mother thinks that they are demons, I do believe that they are part of the legion that is the egregore emanating from the Devil.

Angela Marie is an Astrologer from Connecticut. Her journey in metaphysics started at the age of 15 when she began as an apprentice in Watertown. Her quarter century of experience and intuitive approach to Astrology and Tarot reading, paired with her passion for helping others understand life's paths, are some of the many reasons she has become one of the most trusted and sought-after astrologists in Connecticut.

How does Angela find answers? Her approach to readings utilizes several fundamental practices including Astrology, Tarot, Numerology & lightwork, plus her abilities as a Medium. This benefits the person being read as Angela uses every possible resource to offer a very genuine and honest perspective into one's life.

ONE TWISTED NIGHT AT THE TWISTED VINE RESTAURANT

by Margaret Scholz

One evening, a friend and I went to an investigation at the Twisted Vine restaurant in Derby, Connecticut. While there I investigated several of the alleged "hot spots" in the building, including the basement and the attic. Several people on the investigation were getting great evidence. I, however, was not. I decided to join my friend and some of the others who were checking their cameras and recorders in the main dining area.

While sitting there checking out the photographs that I and others had taken, we all heard a little girl giggling from the balcony above us. We all looked towards the balcony, and then at each other asking "did you hear that?" The interesting part is that there were no young children there at that time.

Margaret Scholz, who also has another chapter in the book, has lived in Milford, Connecticut for almost 37 years. She has been interested in and has investigated the paranormal since 2001 after working in a haunted store in Milford. Margaret was a member of a couple of paranormal groups over the years but has since gone out on her own.

PHANTOM MESSAGES OF CONNECTICUT

by Bill Hall

Calls from an Abandoned Office in Bridgeport, CT (2010)

Bob is not involved with the paranormal. After his father died, he received a call from the General Electric service shop where his dad worked for 35 years. That sounds normal, but there is a twist; the shop closed soon after his father retired. The call originated from his father's old extension, 2618. The building was completely empty, and for security purposes, General Electric bolted all the exits shut and turned off the phone and electrical service. Bob told us, "I have no idea what happened. I am content thinking that Dad might just be saying hello to his boy."

The fact that the calls are coming from his dad's old extension is interesting. It could be a technological explanation because his dad did not talk on the call. In any event, it's a wonderful and charming story and we agree with Bob. Who knows? It is nice to think it might be Dad. Perhaps he's listening in another universe?

Vanishing Patient from Room 18 in Vernon, CT (2003)

Jen didn't know her grandmother well. Being adopted, neither did her mother. Nevertheless, she always seemed to be watching over them. In 2003, Jen's mother visited a psychic named Naomi. She didn't provide much information, other than a message that was "coming through" particularly strong.

Naomi saw a tall, dark-haired woman holding a baby. Jen's mother interpreted that to be her mother, and the baby her sister. While still a baby, her sister tragically drowned in the bathtub. The psychic told her the lady was giving one message: "Life is not long, life is short." The dark-haired woman pointed at her mom while delivering the message.

Fast forward to 2010. Jen was 37 and working as a phlebotomist in a trauma center at St. Luke's Hospital in Cedar Rapids, Iowa. "We often received alerts from the overhead speaker system for stroke land sepsis alerts. When you heard those messages, you immediately hurried to the room that generated the alert. Usually, the room is full of medical personnel," Jen explained. One Saturday morning, around 11 AM, Jen received an alert for room 18. When she arrived at the room, something struck her as odd: There were only two nurses, not the usual assembly of emergency assistance. A nurse was in the process of pulling a white sheet up to the patient's chest. The other nurse was at the computer station. Looking at the nurse by the bed, she asked "Am I in the right room?" The nurse said, "Yes. You're right where you're supposed to be." Just then, the nurse walked out of the room. Jen thought that was odd too. Coworkers and friends acted strange. It was almost as if they didn't know her.

Responding to the sepsis alert, Jen prepped to obtain blood cultures. As she went about her routine, she glanced over to the old man on the bed. He was extremely pale, in his 70s, and sported long white hair with a matching white beard. He was unresponsive. Jen could barely see his chest move beneath the sheet. She feared he was close to death. She put the tourniquet tightly onto his arm. He didn't blink; he wasn't looking at all. As she readied the needle for his arm, he suddenly shot up right in the bed and looked into her eyes. Jen put her left hand on his right shoulder and comforted him. "You're in the ER. I just need to do some blood work on you."

He reacted by lifting his left arm and pointing his long bony finger directly at her face and spoke, "You think life is long. It's not. Life is short!"

Settling back down, she drew his blood. Jen explains, "This man came in as a John Doe, so I had to scan his wristband to keep all of his information in the main database. I scanned each test given, so we could later manually enter the results when that information is received back. I sent the blood to the lab through a system of tubes, like the ones the banks used. Still bothered by his cryptic words, I went over to the nurse's station for about ten minutes. The same nurse was there that was in the room earlier with me."

"Hey, Jen, how are you?" she asked. The nurse acted completely different from when they were in the old man's room earlier. Across the hall from there, Jen could see clearly into room 18. There was an empty, freshly made bed. No patient was there.

Jen inquired, "Where is the man that was just in that room? What's going on with him?"

The nurse responded, "He's been gone for three or four hours." That couldn't be. Jen was in that room with the man less than 10 minutes ago! Confused, Jen explained what happened next: "I ran down to the laboratory to check on the samples I sent down there. The cultures, tubes, records—we looked to find them but there was nothing to be found."

In 2011, Jen found herself back in Connecticut working at St. Francis Hospital in Hartford. She suffered a breakup and left her job and house behind. Those were hard times. Jen told us, "I was texting my mom on break at one of the lowest points in my life. A picture of my grandmother was received during our texting conversation." Jen replies, "Mom, that's a great picture of grandma! It's my favorite." Mom texts back, "I didn't send that. I don't even have that picture on my computer or my cell phone!" An instant mystery was before them. Jen knew *she* didn't send the photo. Someone else did. Or no one did? It just showed up. "We never could figure out how that picture appeared on our phones. Knowing what I was going through at the time, I understood this to mean it was my grandmother telling me I'm not alone and everything's going to be okay because she is here with me."

William J. Hall is the author of the paranormal bestseller "The World's Most Haunted House" and also "The Haunted House Diaries." His website is www.HalloftheParanormal.com and he lives in Plainville, Connecticut.

Jimmy Petonito, who has his own chapter elsewhere in this book, has earned the nickname "Mr. Haunted." He resides in Cheshire, Connecticut, and his website is www.MrHaunted.com. This article is excerpted from their 2018 book "Phantom Messages," which is available from Amazon. Reprinted with permission.

ROBBINS SWAMP, EAST CANAAN: BIGFOOT! ONE OF THE SASQUACHIEST PLACES IN CONNECTICUT

by Colin Haskins and the CCIS Team

It is a fact that Robbins Swamp is the largest wetlands in Connecticut. At over 1500 acres and surrounded by incredible amounts of unexplored wilderness, Mount Canaan rises like a sleeping king above the swamp. The finest marble in the world is mined there. As you venture through "Sand Road," you pass houses and farms and a parallel line of old railroad tracks that accompany you along the way. After driving for a while, you encounter big fields with no trails, and only a kiosk marks the location in yellow letters: "Robbins Swamp Wildlife Management Area."

Searching the internet for details only leads to hunting information, so, after receiving some feedback and various reports on the area, we finally decided to explore it. We headed to a plain field with a gate right across the sign and immediately noticed, as we walked, many pieces of pure white marble. The swamp is mineral rich and boasts plentiful wildlife.

CCIS gets many reports of different areas inside and outside Connecticut on a daily basis, and we take every report seriously. After getting an online report and an image from a lady who lived nearby, with a very convincing and huge Bigfoot print photo, we did not hesitate to investigate the area. Since our witness was not too specific about the location where the photo was taken, we were uncertain if we arrived at the right location. To our surprise, we did not only find a Bigfoot print around 16 inches long in the open field used as hunting area but also other strange bipedal canine tracks with a five feet span between each track! There is no way a dog could leave tracks like that! Unless this one was a huge dog that walked standing on his back legs. A "Dogman" perhaps? A weird canine? Many thoughts crossed our minds, but at this point it is hard to know. Robbins Swamp has a vast forge base for predators and that makes the most logical explanation as to why cryptids would prefer it as habitat or temporary home.

Bigfoot Footprint Photo by Colin Haskins

We documented the evidence on video and measured the most significant prints. Sadly, back then, we were not prepared with the proper materials to cast prints for further analysis. We did find several shotgun shells from hunting activity around the open fields, which could explain the many diverse types of tracks found in some of the muddy areas, surrounded by very dense vegetation. We certainly underestimated the potential of this place at the beginning but as we started to roll the camera and walk around, the place started to make more sense.

We often return to this area, as there is so much to explore. If you follow the train tracks parallel to Sand Road, you will discover an abandoned rail car that just oozes creepiness. Go into the adjacent woods and you will find many tree stands, where hunters can go up and check out their prey without being seen (picture a treehouse without walls). I saw huge *Squatch* structures there in one of my visits, it defied all explanations.

I also tried a call tap and did some howls as well, trying to get any possible Bigfoot response. A call tap is a Sasquatchers term for the action of taking a branch and banging it on a tree. That, and hitting two stones together, are some of the ways to communicate with Bigfoots.

I first found out about this place from a DEP agent who was a friend of mine. I asked him if there was any place where he ever felt watched (his job was to visit places like this). He got real quiet for a moment and after giving it a thought he then said: "Robbins Swamp." He recalled how he was deep in the area we visited and got a strange feeling of being watched. He elaborated that he felt so uncomfortable there that he turned around and left. That is when I knew I had to see it for myself.

I must warn you that the oddly flat terrain of Robbins Swamp is thick, the insects and fauna there are dense and gnarly. This is not a place that tourists or day trippers would go to, as it is not comfortable. It has no facilities. At the junction of railroad tracks and Sand Road, there is an unassuming parking area. Across the street is a nondescript agricultural field that leads to a further back second field where the tracks are to be found.

Remember, this is a place where it will be easy to get lost, so be careful and pay attention to the path you take. Anybody searching for cryptids should make this trip.

Do not forget to be ready for an encounter. After all, you'll never know what you could find. As I always say: *"It's about getting out there!"*

Colin Haskins is a poet from Lubec, Maine. As an active poetry event promoter, he dedicated his life to creating new exciting events locally and throughout the world to bring poets and artists together for a common goal. Haskins is the creator and host of the online show: "CCIS-On Location and Field Investigations" by the Connecticut Cryptid Investigative Society, which he founded. Haskins and his research team explore and investigate the unknown and discover new places in search of cryptids. You can join and follow his adventures on the CCIS Facebook page, YouTube channel, Instagram, TikTok, and Twitter. CCIS has visited, documented, and explored many wildlife and recreational areas putting both known and unknown places on the map for hikers, explorers, and/or sasquatch lovers. CCIS offers a fun, entertaining way of seeing cryptids, following up sighting reports, and and showing around Connecticut diversity, as they search for cryptids. Connecticut Cryptid Investigative Society Fanpage: https://www.facebook.com/CTCryptid. Group: https://www.facebook.com/groups/CTCryptid

SEASIDE SHADOWS

by Rich Cyr

My interest in the paranormal began at an early age. I was hooked when I saw the movie *Poltergeist* in 1982. I soon began reading books on the phenomenon and started attending lectures from the pioneering paranormal power couple Ed and Lorraine Warren. I attended so many of their lectures that I eventually became friends with the two of them.

Lorraine invited me over to their house in Monroe, Connecticut to check out their museum of artifacts that they collected over the years, including the infamous Annabelle doll.

My interest never waned, and I would go on many ghost tours all around Connecticut, Massachussettes, and Rhode Island. Everywhere I went I would take pictures, hoping to catch some kind of entity or any example of paranormal activity. When I first began, I used disposable cameras. The next day I would rush to the local photo mart hoping to see if I captured anything on film. Besides a few orbs I never did get anything significant, even when I attended the *Dracula Tour to Transylvania* in 2005 (presented and hosted by the author of this book, Charles F. Rosenay!!!).

My travel and explorations continued, with little or no results until 2016, when I went on the *Seaside Shadows Haunted History Tour* in Mystic, Connecticut. The tour featured a walk around the city stopping at places that are considered haunted. One such place was an old house where a story is told as follows: "Back in the Civil War period two young boys were killed in this house. At the time of their death, both were lively, fun, and energetic." According to our tour guide their love of life continued even after death. They loved to appear for passersby. I immediately began taking pictures with my cell phone. Looking closely, I saw an image that I couldn't quite make out in the left corner of a doorway's windowpane. I zoomed in to where the image was. Clear as day were two small boys smiling.

To ensure that it wasn't something that could be misconstrued as a flash, which I never used, I double-checked to confirm that the flash was off the entire time. I ended up taking 15 to 20 more pictures from across the street, where the original was taken and closer to the door.

However, that one single photo is the only one that featured the two boys. I even looked inside to see if anyone was in there. It was a small room where no one could hide. The room was empty.

I have told this story and brought this picture to many paranormal conventions where investigators wanted me to send it to them to see if they might find an answer of what it might be. None could find another explanation.

To this day, I don't think that it's a coincidence that the photo I took matches the story being told. This picture is proof that paranormal activity is real.

The Two Boys. Photo by Richard Cyr

The Two Boys. Enlarged and enhanced. Photo by Richard Cyr

Rich Cyr is a musician, radio host, stand-up comedian, actor, author, voice actor, motivational speaker, and podcaster. In his early twenties, Rich was the lead singer for several bands. They played all over the state of Connecticut, selling out most shows. Realizing that he wasn't making enough money to support himself, he enrolled into Connecticut School of Broadcasting. This led to working as a disc jockey at several major radio stations, including the now defunct 106.9 WCCC. When the last station he worked at was bought out, he decided to try stand-up comedy. In just four years he performed over 400 times in nine different states. The biggest was at the world famous "Zanies" in Nashville, Tennessee, performing in front of a sold-out crowd opening for comedian Jeff Ross.

In 2018 Rich wrote his first book, "Confessions of A Frenetic Mind: 5 Tales of Blood Curdling Terror." During this time, he was asked to be on the radio show "Nutmeg Junction," which pays homage to the old-time radio serials such as "The Shadow" and "Flash Gordon." With all original scripts he lends his voice on a show that is currently heard on fifteen stations, including one in Canada and New Zealand. This radio show led to taking over hosting duties of the companion interview show 'Nutmeg Chatter.' Rich is known for his in-depth interviews due to his extensive research. Past guests include Dee Wallace, Adrienne Barbeau, Victoria Price (Vincent's daughter), Anne Serling (Rod's daughter), Charles F. Rosenay!!!, and many more.

Due to the pandemic Rich was no longer allowed to have guests in the studio, so he created a YouTube channel, which led to the creation of two new shows: 'The CLAW's Corner' and 'The Local Artist Show.' They can now be seen all over the world as well as being heard on five radio stations.

Rich has acted in several movies, and can be seen portraying Beetlejuice and The Grinch at The Strand Theater in Seymour, Connecticut. In 2021 Rich's life story was staged at The Palace Theater in Waterbury, Connecticut. The show was entitled, '2nd Act,' in which he discussed the many achievements that he accomplished throughout his life. It was a sold-out performance.

SEYMOUR: A DIFFERENT KIND OF HOWLING

by Diane Berti

As a child, I was sensitive to things around me that others didn't seem to be able to perceive. My family home growing up in Seymour was the hotspot for many of these paranormal occurrences, and it took many years before I felt comfortable relaying this story to my parents. I recall a dog clattering around the house on a chain. We never owned a dog, so, more often than not, the presence was a surprise to me.

During the night, I would hear the dog slowly making its way through the house, until it eventually settled next to me in bed. The weight of it was enough to make the bed sink down in the spot where it would lay. In the morning, I would see new damage on the walls where the chain ground them down.

As I got older, I eventually moved out of the house. Periodically, I would go home and visit my parents. I noticed that the entity had changed at this point. It manifested at this point as a strong, lonely, emotional pull down into the lower basement, as if begging someone to come down and pet it, but when I would go look for it, it was gone.

Outside of House. Photo by Diane Berti

It wasn't until a few years ago that I finally told my parents about this dog. My father, predictably, didn't notice anything and brushed my story off. However, my mother and brother both had stories about this exact same entity and how it would crawl through the house and lay next to them, and later would be a powerful emotional weight that was borderline oppressive. It latched on to anyone it could target!

It eventually got to the point where we were forced to banish it, and thankfully, as of this writing, it hasn't come back.

Diane Berti is a medium and is co-owner of Connecticut Paranormal and Supernatural Tracking Society. She was born and raised in Connecticut.

STRATFORD'S PORTAL LADY

by Nick Grossmann

Several years ago, after conducting a very successful psychic event at the Fright Haven haunted attraction in Stratford, Connecticut, I received a phone call from Charles F. Rosenay!!!, who has since become my partner in many paranormal projects. He is the reason this book exists, and he was responsible for one of my scariest, most dangerous, and most memorable paranormal cases.

A woman with deep troubles had reached out, requesting help with the belief that she had a powerful entity in her home. Coincidentally, her home was in Stratford, Connecticut. She was frazzled and needed assistance desperately. Talking to her on the phone in our first conversation, I could hear the fear and confusion in her shaking voice. Not to mince words, she was terrified.

We arranged a time to visit her. It was me, along with Jeffrey Gerry and Diane Berti of CT PASTS.

I remember walking into the small home not feeling quite right. In fact, I was sure that there was a strong supernatural presence there. We proceeded to interview the women in great detail. She reported that the entity's name was Robert and that he touched her. When I pressed her for more specifics, she revealed some very private and frightening insight. She talked in detail of a spirit that would sexually assault her, throw her off the bed, give her black eyes, and more. She was very explicit, and it was chilling to hear all the graphic incidents. You name it, and it was done to her. I must confess that I suspected mental illness, but that may be part of me going in with a skeptical mind.

Most of the time, in our Nutmeg State, I get blown away by the hauntings we have here.

On the first night we went and interviewed her, nothing happened besides what she told us, but we did have our own feelings of a strong ominous presence. We also registered some disrupted electromagnetic energy or static, but nothing significant.

When we returned there a second time, we felt that the best method for determining what we may be dealing with was by conducting a seance. We put the EMF meter right in front of our client. It wasn't long before she yelled out "Get out of me!," and when she said that, the EMF meter shot up beyond any digital number I have ever seen on it before or since. We were now coming to a theory that we were potentially dealing with what is called an incubus. We felt that this lady may have accidentally summoned it. People with even slight mental conditions don't realize that they can manifest spirits that they believe in. We were almost positive that this was the case here. Also, if individuals are lonely, sometimes they welcome in the spirits now knowing the inherent danger. If they're very lonely, they'll also call in a number of paranormal teams, although not necessarily to rid themselves of the incubus or entity, but rather to have company. We're not psychiatrists or psychologists, nor are we saying that was what was going on with this woman, but we are just suggesting the possibilities. No matter what, she was possessed in one form or another.

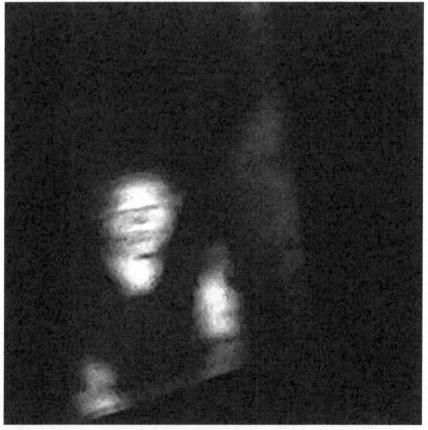

Photo by Jeffrey Gerry

After the EMF incident, Jeff was taking many photos. Suddenly, out came an entity with no eyes chasing us. He captured it on film before we freaked out and fled from that room. He was the height and demeanor of a young teen. When I looked into the living room, I saw the entity on the couch appear and then quickly vanish.

This wasn't an easy process, nor a quick one. We spent a good six months at her place (not so *good*, come to think of it). This haunting was unlike anything we ever dealt with. Often in paranormal investigations you must go back multiple times or try numerous remedies. Or a series of repeated attempts with variations. We thought we tried everything. After much consideration and by process of elimination, we decided to perform a ritual wherein I extract the entity while my colleagues trap it in a bottle. We did this, and then took the bottle (sealed with wax) to my haunted artifacts museum.

The next day the lady reported that the spirit was gone.

She was very pleased and told us that we accomplished what other teams and individuals could not. We were equally pleased with the results, confident that this was a closed case.

We didn't hear from her for a month or so, but then I got a voicemail from her, saying, "Nick—I need your help again... He's back." I remember feeling very frustrated, and sick to my stomach. I wondered if she willed it back. We returned and she admitted that when Robert was gone, she missed him. We didn't know if we succeeded or not, and whether she'd invited a different presence into her existence or the same one, but we were disappointed.

We returned to her home and she showed us a video. The place had been wired with cameras. We could only assume she had invited yet another team in to analyze her situation. Was this just her being lonely? One would have thought so, but no! One video showed a giant spider-like entity with tentacles. We wondered if we were dealing with a shapeshifter/incubus. Jeff concocted a cleansing potion, and I went up into the attic with it. I couldn't believe what I saw next. The area was laden with giant, thick spider-like webs. They were so heavy that if you had asthma, you would probably suffocate if they wrapped around you. I admit I was scared, mostly because I was in that attic numerous times before, and there were never webs there prior to this night. I don't like spiders to begin with, so you can imagine how I felt about an area full of them that may have been supernaturally charged, or whatever it was. I sprayed the formula all over the attic. I then proceeded to go downstairs and spray the rest of the house.

After about five minutes into the cleansing, we started hearing banging and rumbling in the attic. Obviously, whatever it was hated the potion. We repeated this on four separate occasions in a two-week period, but it didn't cure the scenario. Our own cameraman, Hector, caught on video a set of glowing eyes staring at us outside the door and blinking, which we still have recorded.

That night I went home, and while lying in my bed, it began to shake. I jumped out of the bed thinking there was an earthquake, but the shaking stopped. The scariest part of all was right after that. I went to the bathroom to turn on the faucet to wash my face, and the water that came out was blood red. I did not dream this. Needless to say, I was freaked out because that's never happened to me before.

Frustrated, we went back to her house in Stratford. Was her home a portal into something evil? Was the woman herself the portal? I surveyed her house very carefully and asked her why she never invited us to examine her outside shed. She was reluctant for some reason. This time I convinced her to let us in, and inside we found an old cardboard box. When we opened it, in the box was this piece of stained glass which may or may not have emanated from a church or Freemason's

Photo courtesy Nick Grossmann

lodge. She said we can take it away, so I wrapped it carefully and brought it back to lock it up and display it in my museum. I keep it there sealed in a glass case surrounded by three crucifixes. The EMF meters still show spikes from it, and the EVPs still get demonic recordings. Some say the countenance on the stained glass is not of a holy cleric, but rather an angry, blasphemous man who has broken the Ten Commandments and is ready to cast spells contrary to those commandments. See and judge for yourself.

Removing the stained glass did the trick. We would never have known. She has never complained of any visitations again. As of this date, that is.

THE EGYPTIAN CRYPTID THAT ESCAPED NEW HAVEN'S CENTER CHURCH CRYPT

by Chrystyne McGrath

My name is Chrystyne McGrath, and I clear non-beneficial energies. I am a natural born medium, and both of my sons are gifted as well.

In 2015, I was in the crypt under Center Church in New Haven. The headstones still remain, as the foundation of the church was built around it. While there, I saw the spirit of the original minister and his wife. He was telling me that he was upset that the church had put a vent and airway above his headstone.

There were spirits of children near the wall as well. But nothing was as jarring as when I saw a weird four-legged cryptid. As well as being scary and on all fours, it was from Egypt. It had attached itself to an artifact that was brought to Yale in New Haven. It was attracted to the energy of the green which still has thousands of bodies interned. The New Haven Green served as a cemetery from 1638 to 1794. The

Photo Credit: centerchurchonthegreen.org

crypt in the center of the green has layers of bodies within it. This Egyptian Cryptid ended up in the crypt and that's where I came across it. I could feel its unloved energy, it was of a low vibration.

I went home to my house in Guilford, and it had attached itself to me. My two sons were home, and my older son had a friend from high school over. As we were in the living room, my younger son, who was seven years old at the time, went down on all fours. We watched his skin go gray and he started growling. I knew right away the cryptid had got on him and was trying to take over his body. I picked him up and ran outside with him. In the driveway I began to perform an exorcism on my son with holy water, sage, and religious items. It came out of my son and went into the woods.

My son's skin came back to its normal color and he was freaked out. My older son and his friend were so scared as they had witnessed the entire event. I had an Egyptian ring with the symbol of protection overnighted. I continue to use it to clear any old Egyptian energy.

Words do not work when communicating with a non-human energy—only symbols work.

As a footnote to this, my son's friend did not go to the high school and tell everyone what happened. I thought we might have to move!

Chrystyne McGrath is a Trance Medium, Psychic, Reiki Master, Energy Healer, Master Dowser, Ordained Minister, and Teacher. She is the founder of CM Paranormal Services. Chrystyne has over 25 years of experience in Energy Healings, Readings, and Clearings. She has healed thousands of people with her gifts that she was born with. She does this through her intuition, clairvoyance, and healing hands. Chrystyne believes we are pure forms of energy, and that we must take care of our energy just as we take care of our physical bodies. She heals people through her Readings and many sessions that she offers. Chrystyne offers in person, phone, Facetime, Zoom, or Skype Readings. Visit: www.chrystynemcgrath.com

THE HOSPITAL

by Kathy Chruszcz

I am a person who has always preferred the night. I love when it gets dark early in the day, and I am a self-professed "night owl." When I passed my nursing boards and began working in the nursing field, I opted to work the night shift. Not only is it more serene; it allowed me to spend more time with my patients when they were in need as opposed to the busy day shift. I began working at a Bridgeport, Connecticut hospital in the oncology unit, as well as for a local rehabilitation/nursing home.

I had a great uncle who we all were very close to. He was very kind, giving, and just a truly wonderful man. He had an uncanny resemblance to the famous motion picture actor Burt Lancaster, and would get mistaken for him all the time. Unfortunately, his diabetes had caught up with him, and he had surgery to remove one of his limbs below the knee, and this required after-care at rehab.

He was admitted to the facility where I was employed into the private "observation" room across from the nurse's station. I was happy he was there so I could keep an extra eye on him.

After a few weeks, his other limb began to show signs of failure and his health had declined rapidly. The family decided he was too frail to endure another surgery. He was put on comfort measures and passed peacefully a few days later.

I had come back to work to find one of our regular residents now in the room that my great uncle had previously occupied. Her name was Flo, and was a ninety year old woman with Alzheimer's who recently had a fall and broke her hip. She was a very lovely woman and a pleasure to have as a patient.

One night, one of the nurse's aides took me aside and told me she thought Flo, despite her Alzheimer's, had psychic abilities. I asked her why she thought this, and she told me that Flo said that her mother in Jamaica misses her and she should call her. I explained to her that Flo was a lovely lady and that she was probably just going off of the aide's Jamaican accent, encouraging her to check in with her mother.

Photo by Anthony Mullin, East Coast Paranormal Photography

I didn't think anything else of this until I had to check Flo's vital signs an hour later. When I walked in the room, I found her awake and asked if she had trouble sleeping. She said, "No, I can't sleep because there is a man sitting in that chair over there. Why do you allow men to come in my room and sit in my chair?"

I assured her we did not let these kinds of things happen. I went over to the chair and sat it in and suggested maybe she mistook it for the shadows coming in through the window. I got up from the chair, and she replied, "No, he's there, and as soon as you got up, he sat right back down!" She was very adamant about this, so I asked her what the man looked like. "He looks like Burt Lancaster, but I know it's not him because Burt Lancaster still has his legs. This man is missing his leg, and he is telling me his name is Gil."

My great uncle's name was Gil. I couldn't believe what I was hearing, and I excused myself from the room to take in this information. Flo had been on a different floor when my uncle was here for the short time he was and didn't know he was a patient at the facility. She would never even have come in contact with him. What other way would she have this information? This was many years before I realized I had psychic gifts. Despite many years of being involved in paranormal investigating, this incident really shook me up, and still does.

I gathered myself and went back into her room and asked her how she was feeling. She told me, "That guy is still here and he's keeping me up. Can you please tell him to leave?" I told her that I would take care of the situation. I came back with a sleeping pill she was ordered to have if she had problems with insomnia and gave it to her. As I was leaving, I "pretended" to tell "the man" that he had to leave and told her that he was gone. "Good riddance to him!!!," she said as I was turning off her over bed light and adjusting the covers.

I returned to the nurse's station and thought about my great uncle for a while. I said some prayers for his well-being and asked God to look after him and help him cross over. After my shift, I went home and slept for sixteen hours straight as I felt drained and exhausted.

I had a few days off from work. When I returned, I asked Flo if she had seen the man in her room since the other night. "No. Whatever you said did the trick and he's not bothered me anymore." I told her I was glad and from that night in she never mentioned him again.

I have since had my psychic awakening and I now understand. I believe I needed to be there as a conduit to help my uncle pass over, as well as to comfort Flo. It was an experience I will never forget because it was so close to home for me.

Over the years, I have had numerous similar experiences, and only when experiencing my psychic awakening years later on did I begin to understand why these things happen.

Kathy Chruszcz was born in Bridgeport, Connecticut and was interested in the paranormal at an early age. In 2000, she moved to Dublin, Ireland and Somerset, England, and investigated many places in the UK, and other areas, including Dracula's Castle in Transylvania, Romania. Kathy had her psychic awakening on September 11, 2011. She relies on all five senses to commune with the other side and has given readings to people that have helped them gain answers to the questions they sought. She finds her gifts seem to be evolving every day.

THE LITCHFIELD SLAYING

by Betsy-ann Rosenberg

In the mid-eighties, two former customers of the antique shop where I worked opened their own shop. It was in an old plaster house along a main route in the Litchfield County area of Connecticut.

My husband and I stopped in one day to see their new place. It wasn't long after entering the fieldstone storage area that we stepped into the house itself. Immediately inside the door, I stopped in my tracks.

My husband is quite accustomed to my sensitivity to spirit and residual energies, so he wasn't surprised by my next question, but the owners were a bit shocked.

"I'm sorry, but did someone die here?" I asked. They looked at each other, and their faces seemed to go white. After a moment, they explained that not too many years before, someone had indeed died on the exact spot where I was standing. I explained about my clairvoyance and sensitivity, then related what I felt and what I "saw."

Looking down, under (and "through") the rug I was standing on, was a dark stain. I sensed the figure of a man where I stood. On the set of stairs immediately to my right, approximately six steps up, a young man stood frozen. His arms at his side, he was looking down. I did not see a weapon but I knew he had one.

They then told me a man was shot there, in a drug-related incident. I did reassure them that there were no malevolent spirits present, just residual energies left because of the shock of what happened, a sad imprint embedded in the house's "memory."

A Spiritualist Intuitive card reader for over 45 years, Betsy-ann Rosenberg has been sensitive to spirits since childhood, and often has mediumship experiences during her card readings. Messages may be received via clairvoyance, clairaudience, clairsentience, clairalience, or claircognizance. Over the past 20 years she has become known for her readings and Reiki work through several local Connecticut psychic and 'New Age' fairs as well as the ParaConn (A Momentary Calm). Rosenberg has clients from Connecticut to the Carolinas, offering readings using Gypsy Witch cards and The Gilded Tarot.

Over the years she has been asked to visit various private homes and other buildings, to do space clearings or evaluate energies or activities reported. She can often connect with any spirits and determine their intentions and ask them to either leave or stop disturbing the current occupants. Thankfully they have all been non-confrontational! Besides many years of teaching and customer service, and being a wife, mom, and grandmother, Betsy-ann is also an artist (After Midnight Creations) and Reiki Master.

THE NEW DEMON HOUSE OF DERBY

by Mike Cronin

On a Saturday night in early September of 2021, my team, 2 Brothers Extreme Paranormal, wound up at a private home in Derby, Connecticut. The residence was a short walk from a huge Catholic Church and a smaller Congregational Church.

The owner of the home had met us a few months before at the first ParaConn paranormal convention in nearby Ansonia, Connecticut. She had told us about what happens to her at night while trying to sleep; from feeling suffocation to being physically pulled out of her bed. She related to us that shadow figures were always touching her, or she would be feeling them pass through her.

After her showing us photos and videos from cameras she had set up in her room, which captured her being attacked while sleeping and pillows flipping up on their own, we knew we had to help her.

We arrived at the house at around 7:30 PM to investigate with our colleagues at Team DOA Supernatural. As soon as we entered her bed-

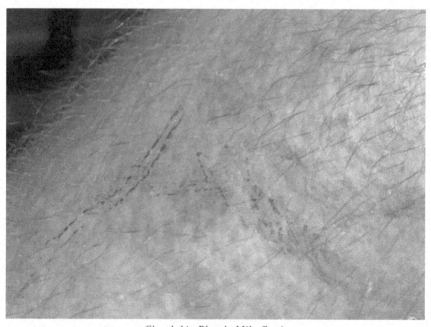

Clawed skin. Photo by Mike Cronin

room to place cameras, we all felt a very heavy feeling, and we all had a hard time breathing. This continued throughout the night. Our SLS camera was active and our other app camera GhostTube kept picking up an entity calling out "Demon," "AntiChrist," and also saying "the owner is hers," and to "get out." Other demonic sayings were coming forth throughout the night as well.

Clearly, we were in a demonically-charged house. As seen in the photo, one of us was clawed while sitting in a possessed chair. The homeowner's son felt rage and constant anger while sitting in the chair. He wasn't imagining it; I felt it too. I decided to do a spirit box session while sitting in the chair to try and find out what did the clawing.

Despite equipment malfunctions throughout the night and other challenges, we recorded a great deal of video evidence.

We ended the night by dousing holy water and sage, along with closing prayers. At 4:30 AM when we walked outside of the house, we realized that the heaviness was lifted from all of us.

All parties, including the homeowners, are safe and everyone is in good spirits. We're not sure all the entities were gone, but we believe the evil forces had been banished.

This was a paranormal night and investigation we will never forget.

2 Brothers Extreme Paranormal is a paranormal investigation team out of Middletown in the Middlesex County section of Connecticut. They investigate private homes and businesses.

When they aren't doing private investigations, the Cronin Brothers are on the road to the most haunted locations on the East Coast, including Eastern State Penitentiary in Philadelphia, Pennsylvania; Salem, Massachusetts (multiple locations); Green Lady Cemetery in Burlington, Connecticut; Fort William Henry in Lake George, New York; Hoosac Tunnel in North Adams,

Massachusetts; Houghton Mansion in North Adams, Massachusetts; Retreat Tower in Brattleboro, Vermont, and many others. Visit them on Facebook, Instagram, and YouTube for info, photos, and videos.

Editor's Note: On another paranormal investigation at this same location in February of 2022, a group visit was organized and hosted by "The Shaman and The Showman." The investigation, conducted by Nick Grossmann of GhostStorm, drew very intense results. The most outstanding was when a metallic ball was thrown in Grossmann's direction from a wall.

THE OLD PINE TREE

by John Zaffis

Connecticut is the Nutmeg State, but there are probably many more pine trees in the state. This is about a case I investigated where the individuals in the family did not follow through with the instructions left behind by the deceased uncle. They had no children of their own so his last request to family members was to follow through with his wishes of being cremated, and his ashes to be spread around an old pine tree in the back of the home.

He had died two years prior to his wife, and she was in failing health at the time. Therefore, she was not up to following through with any of this at the time and put the urn with the ashes in a closet. Her health deteriorated over the next two years, and she completely forgot about the ashes in the urn in the closet. She passed away and the home was put up for sale with a lot of their personal effects left behind—including the urn.

A family purchased the home and was removing a lot of the things left behind. They discovered the ashes and called the family to come and remove the urn out of the home. This was not part of the sale, so the relatives had to remove it. They brought it home with them. Soon after that, the haunting began, and things escalated in the home. Lights would go on and off in the basement where the workbench was with all his tools, and there was an ice-cold spot in the living room where he sat in his favorite chair with the smell of tobacco in certain areas of the home. After talking to the family members, they found out that some of these spots were his favorite areas.

At this time, I began an investigation into the situation and found out that the family did *not* spread the ashes around the big old tree on the property. The tree was cut down and removed for a new septic system and the family did not see any sense in doing this after that. I knew it was time for someone to make contact with the relatives and have them come over to spread the ashes in this area and hope this would resolve the problem at hand.

The family responded and the ashes were spread out in this area where the tree had been as he had requested it. Lo and behold, all the activity stopped, and it all worked out good for the new family. Everything was back to normal. So, as you can see, it is always advisable to listen to the folks' requests at the time they pass away. If we can follow through with the last wishes when we are asked to, this can help with the deceased to pass over and to be at rest with loved ones and family.

John Zaffis has over four decades of experience studying and investigating the paranormal. He worked for—and with—his aunt and uncle, Ed and Lorraine Warren. This sent John beyond looking for ghosts and hauntings and into studying demonology under the Warrens. This led to John's involvement with cases of posses-

sion and exorcism, giving him the opportunity to work with prominent exorcists in this field, including Roman Catholic priests, monks, Buddhists, rabbis, and ministers. His research has taken him throughout the U.S., Canada, and the U.K. covering several thousands of cases.

John has a great deal of first-hand paranormal experience, including experience with ghosts, poltergeists, and demonic and diabolical entities. He has also worked extensively with both spiritualists and psychics concerning how their knowledge is used for channeling, reincarnation (past-life regression), calling of the spirits for information, and how they use meditation to acquire the information which they are seeking. Because of his personal experiences with hauntings, ESP, near death experiences, and other paranormal activities, he is considered one of the foremost authorities in the field today. He stands firm in his conviction that such phenomena exist.

Over the years, John has collected hundreds of possessed items either given to or sent to him by people wishing to be rid of them. The John Zaffis Paranormal Museum opened in 2004 to display these items and continues to be open today. John wrote and starred in the documentary film Museum of the Paranormal, released in 2010, which gives the viewer a tour of his museum and the stories behind some of the objects.

John has been featured in the SyFy television series "Haunted Collector" (2011-2013), Discovery Channel's documentaries "A Haunting in Connecticut" and "Little Lost Souls." He has also appeared on "Unsolved Mysteries," on Piers Morgan, and numerous print and news media events. John has also appeared on "Ghost Hunters" and "Ghost Adventures." He appears in "Graveyards" and "In A Dark Place," both books written by Ed and Lorraine Warren. John's first book, "Shadows of the Dark," co-written with Brian McIntyre, was released in September of 2004. He is working on multiple follow-up books and is lecturing all over the United States including colleges and universities.

THE PINK LADY OF NEW HAVEN

by Charles F. Rosenay!!!

In the seventies and eighties, a section of New Haven near Grand Avenue not far from Clinton Avenue was home to the legend of the "Pink Lady." I had forgotten about her/it until I began compiling the stories for this book.

Ed DiPiazza, my best friend in college, asked me if I knew about the Pink Lady. Ed and I worked together at the college radio station, where I would talk about The Beatles and The Monkees, and he would rave about Bruce Springsteen and The Who, especially Keith Moon, who he resembled. He was surprised that I hadn't ever heard about the Pink Lady, and he told me we were going to visit her someday.

In the early 1980s, there was a really bad musical television variety show on NBC called *The Pink Lady and Jeff*, which was short-lived and deservedly so. Being the pop-culture nerd that I am, just like Dudleytown made me think of Dudley Do-Right, the legend of the Pink Lady made me think of that abysmal TV program.

Boy, was I in for a surprise.

Ed told me very little about what was in store, but I was able to get a hint that there was some sort of supernatural element to all of this. I'd never been on a ghost-hunt before, the word "paranormal" wasn't part of my vocabulary yet, but I was a horror kid and loved anything scary, so I was certainly up for whatever adventure my friend had in mind.

He hadn't mentioned it in a while, but one weekend night we had finished seeing a band at a New Haven venue, and despite it being very late at night (or perhaps because of it), Ed suggested we visit the Pink Lady. I was up for it, and before I could get my bearings as to where we were driving, Ed pulled the car over to a stop under a bridge. Was this where a person jumped to their death? Did someone lose their life by being hanged off this bridge? Did passengers die when a vehicle plunged off the side of the bridge?

None of the above.

It helps to know that this was a rather seedy part of town. I wasn't very familiar with this neighborhood. It was dark, grungy, and felt like it could definitely be a high crime area. Before I even knew what was going on, I was already feeling uneasy. Ed had turned off the engine, shut off the car lights, and proceeded to tell a campfire story with no campfire in sight.

He talked slowly and thoughtfully, telling me the story of a young New Haven couple who were very much in love. It was the early 1940s, and they had been newly married. The couple found their dream house, and moved into their new home to live happily ever after. That dream was put on hold when the husband was called off to war. Before he left his new wife, he swore that he would soon return, and that he would come around the bend, put on the brights of his car and she would know that he returned to her. She vowed that she would come to the window in her pink gown, and they would continue their love ever after.

Man makes plans, and war sometimes has other endings. We don't really know the ending, but I knew then and there that Ed had started his car back up again and we were driving ahead very slowly.

I'm not completely clear about this part of the story. Nobody knows if our bride went crazy. We don't know if she killed herself, or just died of a broken heart. We don't even know when she died. We do know that her husband never returned.

As we pulled around the bend, Ed pointed to an old, run-down house that looked like it had been long abandoned. He told me to look at the top, corner window as he came to a stop and turned on his high beams. This was it.

It's rare when a ghost ever appears; it's even more rare when one appears on command.

As soon as his bright lights went on, a spectral body wearing a pink nightgown seemingly floated to the window, peered out with large, blank eyes, and disappeared back into the blackness it came from. I actually saw the Pink Lady.

I woke up my parents to tell them all about this. I told all my friends and anyone who would listen. The very next night I brought my parents. This time I drove, parked under the bridge, told the story, and followed the same path. When I made my way around the bend, slowed down to a stop, and turned on my brights, the Pink Lady appeared again. I looked across to see if someone might have been projecting the image, but there were no buildings on the other side of the street. My Mom, who was never quiet, was silent. They couldn't believe it!

They had me go again the next night with one of their friends. The next weekend I brought a few of my friends. That year, whenever I went there, the Pink Lady would always come out. New Haven old-timers knew about the Pink Lady, and the story. After a while I pretty much forgot about her and her story, and more recently, when I tried to find the house again, it was demolished, along with most of the neighborhood. Few people I tell this to have heard about New Haven's Pink Lady.

She never had her "happily ever after," but nobody knows if she ever passed over to her "ever after."

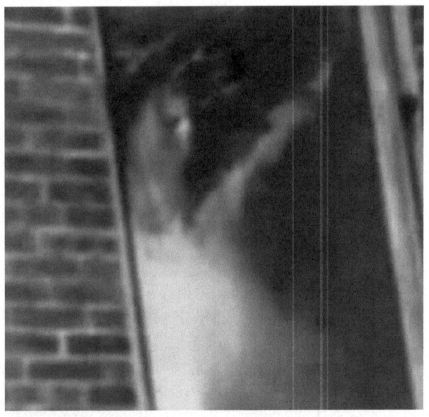

This is not a photo taken of New Haven's Pink Lady described in this chapter. There are no known pictures of her; however, we welcome any. This is simply one of several "pink lady" images on the internet.

AND FINALLY...

Now that you've come to the end, you're saying to yourself that YOUR story would have fit well into this book. I agree.

You don't have to be a paranormal investigator, clairvoyant, or medium. You don't even have to be a writer. You just had to have had that one experience…

It's the one that will stay in your mind forever. It's the one you always think of first when people ask you your most memorable paranormal or unexplained encounter.

It's the one that you think of if anyone asks you if you "believe in ghosts."

You may have a location that nobody has ever been spooked at, or even heard of.

I am hereby asking you to write to me about that ONE memorable, outstanding, scary, unbelievable event or location.

I don't care how long or short it is, or how bad your grammar may be. It just has to have its roots in Connecticut, and it has to be true.

If you would like to be included in the next book, please write it up and email back to ParanormalConnecticut@gmail.com. If you have photos to accompany it, that would be a definite plus.

If you want to include a short bio and photo of yourself (and/or your organization, if there is one), that would be most welcome. If you wish to remain anonymous, that's fine too.

See you in the next book. Or in the next life.

www.ParaConn.org

www.SalemParaCon.org

www.DracTour.com

www.GHOSTOURS.com

www.TheShamanAndThe Showman.com

www.BOOKOFTOP10HORRORLISTS.com

INDEX

2 Brothers Extreme Paranormal.........138
Annabelle Doll.................................99
Ansonia Opera House....................62, 65
Ansonia, CT.................................. 138
Berti, Diane.......................101, 123, 125
Bigfoot..115
Bridgeport, CT...........................112, 132
Burlington, CT................................79
Carousel Gardens............................ 29
Chris Mark Castle............................ 34
Chriuszcz, Kathy............................ 132
Commodore Hull Theatre................... 60
Conjuring House............................105
Conn. Paranormal Research Team....... 35
Cronin, Mike.................................138
Curtis House...................................85
Cyr, Rich..................................... 119
Dark Siege..................................... 40
Davroe, A.L.....................................85
Derby, CT................. 43, 53, 57, 111, 138
DiCarlo, Rich................................... 43
DiPiazza, Ed.................................. 144
DiPietro, Anthony........................... 101
Dracula Tours..................................17
Dreivers, Tommy.............................79
Dudleytown, CT............................ 68, 71
East Coast Paranormal Photography.... 97
East Granby, CT............................103
Elward, Larry and Debbie...........103, 105
Fairfield Hills Asylum.......................... 74
Febus, Joey....................................97
Felix, Richard............................. 18, 46
Fright Haven.................................. 21
Garabo, John.................................. 32
Gerry, Jeffrey......................89, 101, 125
Ghosts of Derby.............................. 53
Green Lady.................................... 47
Green Lady Cemetery.......................79
Grossman, Nick......... 20, 65, 71, 74, 98, 125
Hall, Bill...................................... 112
Haskins, Colin............................... 115
Hieber, Leanna Renee.......................85
Hookman's Cemetery....................... 89
Houdini, Harry................................ 45
Hoye, Katie....................................97
James Furniture Building................... 57
Jodoin, Christopher..........................35
Kreskin, Amazing............................. 11
Levine, Danny................................. 98
Litchfield Slaying............................136
Longo, Paul, Jr................................81
Marie, Angela................................ 108
Mascolo, Michael James.....................57
McGrath, Chrystyne.........................130
McKinney, Lisa Marie....................... 68
McLaughlin, Linda and Kelly................40
McLeod, Jason.................................40
Middletown CT Valley Hospital........... 95
Middletown, CT.............................. 95
Monroe, CT.........................41, 98, 119
Mullin, Anthony...............................95
Mystic, CT....................................119
New-Gate Prison............................103
New Haven, CT....................... 130, 144
New Haven's Center Church............. 130
Nova Scotia Hill............................. 108
Old Pine Tree................................141
ParaConn.......................................23
Peer, Christine and Daniel...................34
Petonito, Jimmy............................. 29
Phantom Messages.........................112
Pink Lady.................................... 144
Portal Lady...................................125
Prospect, CT................................. 92
Quinn, Eric.....................................36
Robbins Swamp............................ 115
Roque, Hector...............................101
Rosenay, Charles...11, 17, 65, 71, 98, 144
Rosenberg, Betsy-Ann.....................136
Saunders, Steve Biff........................ 92
Schiarffa, Paul and Debbie..................29
Scholz, Margaret...................... 53, 111
Seaside Shadows Haunted History ... 119
Seymour, CT.......................29, 90, 123
Shaman and the Showman...... 22, 71, 98
Sterling Opera House............. 43, 53, 61
Stratford, CT.......................... 81, 125
Tours of Terror................................ 17
Twisted Vine Restaurant...................111
Vernon, CT...................................112
Warren, Ed and Lorraine...29, 92, 98, 119
Watertown, CT.............................. 108
Woodbury, CT.................................85
Woodstock, CT................................34
Wooster, William............................ 29
Zaffis, John............................100, 141